THE POOR CHILDREN

STORIES BY
APRIL L. FORD

sfwp.com

Library of Congress Cataloging-in-Publication Data

Ford, April L.
  [Short stories. Selections]
  The poor children : stories / by April L. Ford.
    pages cm
  Includes bibliographical references and index.
  ISBN 978-1-939650-18-4 (trade paper : alk. paper)
  I. Title.
  PS3606.O718A6 2015
  808.83'1—dc23
                                        2014014557

Published by SFWP
369 Montezuma Ave. #350
Santa Fe, NM 87501
(505) 428-9045
www.sfwp.com

Find the author at www.april-l-ford.com

For the poor children

"The world owes its enchantment to these curious creatures and their fancies, but its multiple complicity rejects them. Thistledown spirits, tragic, heartrending in their evanescence, they must go blowing headlong to perdition."

—Jean Cocteau, *The Holy Terrors*

LAYLA

They bit, they kicked, sometimes they pulled out their own hair in such chunks they left hickey-like marks on their scalps that had to be washed and disinfected and covered with gauze. But they would rip off the gauze and wave it in the other kids' faces, the other kids who had ruined their chances of being touched, of feeling human contact—any human contact at all—by retreating into corners, promising to behave. One time a girl drank an entire bottle of bathroom cleaner during chore hour. Locked herself in the bathroom with a device she had fashioned, quite skillfully, during arts-and-crafts that afternoon. She'd had to improvise the lock, for there were none in rooms where kids could not be supervised. Once there had been a camera in the bathroom, but too many kids had been spied on inappropriately, blackmailed by malignant, underpaid juvenile correctional officers.

Layla swigged the entire bottle of cleaning fluid because she knew it had been watered down. The COs measured the fluid before kids used it to clean, then measured it again after chores were done. A drop less than expected was cause for reprimand: an hour in the "quiet room", the evening without privileges (chaperoned walk in the razor-wire courtyard, extra glass of apple juice, *et cetera*, *et cetera*). Usually the most well-behaved kid was assigned bathroom duty, and it was considered an honor, a rite-of-passage even, to he or she who got to snap on the heavy-duty rubber gloves and scrub the toilet until all the day's traces of urine, shit, vomit, spit, semen were gone. Anybody off the street would feel at ease to sit on that toilet.

Layla often wished somebody off the street (not an actual street person because the facility was infested with them, but somebody *off* the street in a suit and tie, carrying a briefcase, maybe) would enter the facility just to use the bathroom. But the night she gulped the cleaning fluid like a bottle of warm, acrid beer, she had given up hope that the man with the briefcase would ever come to rescue her. The last time she had seen her father he walked out in the middle of her trial, arms in the air, muttering, excusing himself but he had to answer the page. He was an important doctor, and one of his important clients needed him. His clients paid for their healthcare. So Layla thought she could maybe get to her father more quickly that way, by drinking cleaning fluid, and if not, then at least somebody would have to pay attention to her until the poison was extracted from her body—if that could be done in time— and somebody, maybe Andrea, a mysterious CO in Layla's mind, the only female on the boys' side, would hold her hand while they pumped her stomach. Maybe even touch her hair, wipe damp strands of it from her face while she frothed at the mouth and vomited like a sick dog.

But. Andrea was not there that night, she was at the other facility where boys as young as five were detained for murder—could they call it murder at five?—and at the exact moment when Layla's eyes rolled toward the top of her skull like a pair of foggy marbles, as her face collapsed and contorted from the spasms in her chest, Andrea was handing her notice of resignation to her supervisor (*I can't take it here anymore*) without apology, for how could a person be expected to apologize for refusing to work any longer with boys who had been born with evil black hearts?

"A five-year-old knows it's wrong to throw his baby sister over the balcony."

"But you knew you'd be working with cases like this. Why else would you, would anyone, want to work here?"

"I applied to work with the girls."

"You can't if you resign."

"Then transfer me to the girls' unit or I'm quitting."

It was a bold threat, to quit working at a facility where COs quit regularly and were replaced with ease as insulting as an ex-lover's slap; but Andrea felt, after six months, it was her time to be bold. She detested the little rapists and murderers, the future arsonists and other monsters being preened for society, society's unsuspecting welcome, for it would not know of the records expunged and burned the day these boys came of age. The greatest gift of all, freedom, would be granted to the very little fiends that had invaded the bodies of their helpless eighteen-month-old sisters, pointed guns at their parents and pulled the triggers, captured their neighbors' cats pregnant with kittens and ripped open swollen bellies in visceral excitement and watched the unborn life leak out. While Andrea's peers in graduate school had prepared for careers as researchers, statisticians, professors of criminology, she had acquired knowledge and skills specific to the Clermont Girls' Correctional Facility. CGCF: A maximum-security experiment, a project designed by the government to "truly rehabilitate" young female offenders. It was the sister facility to CBCF, both just ten minutes outside the city, both identical in floor plan and failure to rehabilitate, though Andrea did not know this yet.

"They're just as bad there. Worse," her supervisor said.

Andrea waved her letter of resignation at him, a rotund man of late-fifties who had succeeded in delaying the physical wear that marked the faces of COs after just one year in the system. He was one of them, she thought contemptuously, one of those people who had studied to become a philosophizer of crime, a reticent idealist. And how easy that was! To speculate why four-year-old Eric had, while the parents slept, wedged a knife into his sleeping infant brother's open mouth, wedged the knife so deep the infant could not cry out, for his tiny lungs were perforated. To speculate why eleven-year-old Bryan had attacked his napping mother with a claw hammer because he was sick of seeing her on the couch like a lazy cunt, just like his father was sick of it. Andrea had stopped trying to make her supervisor admit there was nothing at all to speculate about these cases. They were not riddled with psychological enigmas, they were not behavioral jigsaw puzzles; they were kids who knew what they wanted to do, did it, would do it again.

"Are you nervous working with the boys?"

"No. I applied to work with the girls."

"Fine. They're short-staffed in the unit tonight. We'll see how you feel about all of this tomorrow."

By the time Andrea was authorized to transfer to CGCF for the remainder of her shift (only three hours, during which all girls in the facility were asleep), Layla had been admitted to emergency and the regular COs were back on duty.

"Little bitch," the male chided as he and the female updated Layla's docket.

"Maybe this time she actually did it."

"Put us all out of our misery, why doesn't she."

The COs looked up when Andrea cleared her throat, standing at the entrance of the kitchen where they were seated, stained coffee mugs on the table, torn-open box of tea biscuits beside. Andrea smiled, but the COs showed no interest. She helped herself to a tea biscuit, poured day-old coffee into a Styrofoam cup, sat down and inquired about Layla.

The male whistled. "You think you seen it all over there with the boys? Layla's about the sweetest thing we had here. Now what's left are the girls nobody wants, not even this place. Mangy, miserable, violent things. So wretched inside and out makes you never want children. Do you?"

"No."

These COs were the rough-and-tumble kind who knew the second before a kid was going to fly out of control, could suspend a kid in the air by his wrists, dangle him there like a piece of laundry clipped to a clothesline on a blustering day. And Andrea wondered: Had school made her too soft? All those hours she had spent studying, reading "classic cases" would have been better used jogging or jumping hurdles, training privately with a martial artist. These two COs appeared sturdier than lightning-struck tree stumps, expanded into their uniforms, were enlarged by their uniforms, their eagerness to break apart fights and administer discipline evident in the ropey veins of their foreheads and arms.

"Take rooms one to four," the female said, looking to her co-worker.

The male conceded and pointed to a hallway across from the kitchen. There, at the end, was an orange plastic chair like the kind found in high school classrooms, the wooden desk at its side equally infantilizing, and that was where Andrea sat, in a state of bored agitation, until her shift ended three hours later.

The next day her supervisor transferred her permanently to CGCF after she had finished eight hours in the boys' unit. Layla was back by then, humbled by her near-death experience, enabled by a day of nurses and doctors touching her—gently—and asking if she was okay. *Yes I am. Thank you for asking.* She was beautiful, Layla was. Always quick to express remorse after she misbehaved, caused anyone pain or discomfort, though mostly she caused herself the pain and others inconvenience.

"I don't mean to, but sometimes I can't stop myself."

Andrea listened to Layla's story, her confessions, her pleas for validation, but her focus was on *Layla*, beautiful Layla with a prosthetic left leg. Not the whole leg, just up to the calf. The prosthetic was the crass kind that government subsidy afforded—basic, that awful man-made flesh color, like an exploded Barbie limb—even though her father was one of the wealthiest practitioners in the city.

"He's worried I'd be able to run faster with a better leg."

"Let me see if I can help you."

"Don't bother. It'd just get stolen anyway."

Andrea spent the next week studying Layla's case. She could not find information about why the girl was at the facility, only her conditions: two years detention, drug and alcohol therapy, life skills coaching, anger management, one year probation after discharge. The usual. Layla's conditions were to be enforced on her as an adult (she had entered the system at sixteen), though, which suggested a sequence of serious offenses, and Andrea felt both disappointed and relieved to learn that girls weren't favored by the system after all. Her six months at CBCF had exposed her to the ugliest features of humankind, packaged into boys as young as five, and she found comfort in the knowledge that girls could be just as odious. *I never want children. I hate them all.*

And yet, the pinch in her bladder that had persisted for four months was now accompanied by a darkening of her nipples, which still looked pre-pubescent, maybe because Andrea had, in her teens, been afflicted with a hormonal imbalance that denied her the full breadth of puberty. But now her darkening nipples ached when she removed her bra each day after work. Dark, hard little pellets on her slightly raised chest area, where a man could spread his hands and feel the smoothness of Andrea, feel the tightness of her body and indulge, if he wished, in an otherwise strictly unacknowledged desire for youth.

Andrea's third week working with Layla, Layla said one morning at breakfast: "You going to keep it?"

The three other girls from the wing looked at Andrea with expressions ranging from disgust—if they weren't allowed to have babies then why could she?—to exasperation—they would have to get used to another new CO *again*? Anything to complicate their lives, as if living in this shithole wasn't enough!

"Put your knife down, Candy."

Candy smacked her knife back in place, directly to the left of her plate; all the girls had to keep their knives to the left unless granted permission to use them. "I was just going to offer to help out if you didn't want to keep it."

But Andrea would never do such a thing. What was inside her, the four-month-old and growing thing inside her, was somebody else's growing thing, too. And that somebody else, her boyfriend, the father, had rights. No, Andrea did not feel even the most infinitesimal of impulses to seize the knife from Candy and flip it around in her own hands like a precious instrument. It was just a knife, not meant for such things.

"I said put your knife down, Candy."

Candy put her knife down once more and the other girls at the table, not including Layla, yawned obliquely. They were already bored with Andrea's authority; it really didn't matter to them if she was replaced with another CO. But Layla, Layla clicked her tongue with disapproval, smiled temperately, and Andrea felt the first kick—could it kick at only four months?—a small flutter in her lower abdomen made beautiful by the presence of this circumspect girl with a prosthetic leg. *I'll keep it if it's a girl. If it's a girl I'll name it Layla.*

That night Andrea removed her bra slowly, paid close attention to her breasts once liberated from the unsightly garment (the color of Layla's prosthetic leg) with heavy metal clips that chaffed the skin they pressed against all day.

"When are you coming home?" she asked her boyfriend, who had phoned from his overseas conference, phoned every night after Andrea's shift to make sure none of the kids had bitten or kicked, or worse.

"Soon. Everything okay?"

"Just getting used to working with the girls."

"Sure. Congratulations again."

"Thanks." Andrea traced her index finger from her collarbone to her navel, a flushed patch appearing on the sharp, bony cliff of her breastplate. She pinched one brown nipple, then the other, incapable of imagining their potential to be suckled by tiny human lips, to be chewed by gums so soft the pain might go away. *I can't. I cannot name her Layla.* For what if it was born a boy, a boy without arms or without legs, without any limbs at all, without a docket that stated very clearly why he was there and what she had to do with him? What if he threw her cat over the balcony before his fifth birthday because he had seen the tenant on the facing balcony do the same (impossible, of course, because the tenant was an elderly man who never stepped outdoors for fear his white, veiny skin would melt from sun exposure)? What if Bradley didn't like this thing that had grown inside her? Left one day for a conference and never returned, left Andrea to inflate in such an unattractive, grotesque way that she could never again be seen in a bikini, for the plum-colored skids on her breasts and thighs had revealed the ugliness of life, turned her into someone hideous.

"What do you think of the name Layla?"

"That one of your girls?"

"She's got a prosthetic leg."

"Poor thing."

Andrea and Bradley recited loving words, promised unwavering affection, planned a vacation somewhere nice, tropical, distant and remote, hung up. Andrea felt the pinch in her bladder of the past four months tighten; felt the need to urinate so urgently she barely made it to the bathroom. She pressed her hand to her pelvis, a gentle press for it felt like her bladder had become suddenly inflamed, and even though she had to urinate badly the urine came out in a slow, precise stream. Thick. Invisible sickles that made her groan. *Bladder infection?* Unable to stand—worried she would stand only to have to sit again and cradle her pelvis—Andrea grabbed the pen and notepad from the magazine rack beside the toilet and began to list names of boys.

Yellow Gardenias

I was thirteen when I met Earl. Actually I was twelve and three hundred and sixty-four days and actually I had known about him for a long time before that. I had heard so much about him before I saw him for real that I ended up being disappointed when it finally happened. Forever, dad had talked about Earl like he was a wizard or something.

"Magic. It's like *magic* the way he works that metal snake down the pipes and makes everything better than new!"

Earl had a class-four license. That meant he was good enough to fix rich people's toilets and such. One time he unclogged the toilet of an old colonial mansion on Belvedere Road in Westmount, and dad said the owners were so pleased they practically force-fed Earl a gourmet lunch and then had him chauffeured home in a Mercedes. Earl left his junker in front of the mansion like an eyesore because there was no way he was going to pass up the chance to ride in a car with tinted windows and Alpaca gray leather seats. That's what important people did. Later that day dad drove him back to get his junker but it was gone, and when Earl asked the rich people where it had gone to they said, "Towed." They hadn't realized it was his. They had thought it belonged to somebody who might be watching their home to know when the best time to do a break-and-enter was. Earl did his best to be calm and good-natured when he told the rich people they owed him a new truck, but he pretty much lost it when they only offered him the seventy-five bucks it cost to get his old one back from the impound. He yelled at the rich people that his truck had been in perfect condition and if it had been at all damaged during the tow he would sue them for destruction of private property. Dad had to manhandle Earl off the front lawn when he unzipped his workpants and started to piss all over the rich people's gardenias.

I was maybe ten when dad told me that story, and that's pretty much when I decided Earl was a wizard. Only wizards did things like piss on rich people's gardenias and get away with it. I liked to imagine Earl standing heroically in front of those stupid people's mansion, unzipping his pants casually like he was in an alleyway, and sending a stream of glittering piss onto the gardenias. The gardenias would turn up their stupid flowery faces and drink Earl's water like liquid sunrays and whatever they couldn't absorb would crystallize on their petals and forever, day and night, the gardenias would have yellow dewdrops on them. And the value of the mansion would go up so high even the rich people who lived there couldn't afford it so they would put the mansion up for sale, and Earl would buy it and ask me and dad to go live there with him and every morning we would sit on the front lawn with the gardenias and have espressos and biscotti.

Dad and Earl had been friends forever. They had grown up in a town called Valleyfield, much more west and rural than the city outskirt place I grew up in called Verdun. Actually I was born in Valleyfield, too, but shortly after that mom had a nervous breakdown so the three of us moved to Verdun so she could be close to the Douglas Hospital where she had to stay two weekends every month. Dad wanted Earl to come with us because the police were after him, but mom said she didn't have the stamina to hide a convicted criminal..Earl could hide until he rotted, she said, but the second he poked his head out the door the cops would slap on the handcuffs and cart him off to jail. So what good would it do to hide him? He'd probably be better off at Bordeaux anyhow. The place was ruled by the Angels, and Earl came from a second-generation Hell's family. He'd get good care while he was in there—three square meals a day, a free weight room and swimming pool, a library with as much "T and A" as intellectual stuff, and Movie Night Tuesdays monitored by cute college girls who fantasized about having convict boyfriends.

Earl went and turned himself in after mom told him all that, but he was actually wanted for something bigger so they sent him to the Kingston Penitentiary for nine years. That was where he got his plumber's license, which was why he was let out after nine years instead of fifteen. He had proved he was smart and rehabilitated and anyways the prison needed to make room for criminals that would bring it more money. Dad said Earl was just a regular criminal type, and the newspapers and TV stations didn't pay prisons for interviews with common men. The moneymakers were men like Bernardo. Dad said Earl had known Paul on the inside.

Whenever I asked dad about Valleyfield he said the same thing: It was a dead place where all boys did was race motorbikes on weekends while their girlfriends waited at Tim Hortons and argued nervously with each other about whether or not the marshmallows in their hot chocolates were making them fat.

"No difference," dad would declare, crumpling his forehead like his favorite *Law & Order* agent. "One marshmallow, one hundred marshmallows, no marshmallows at all. Valleyfield girls are just fat."

"But I'm in actuality a Valleyfield girl," I once worried, while dad made us hot chocolates with jumbo-sized colored marshmallows.

"No way, Sammy!" he practically yelled, as he piled an extra marshmallow into my mug. "You're a Jennings and pure and beautiful and skinny! Just like your mother..."

Mom. Dad got all drifty and contemplative whenever the subject of her came up. Most times he was the one to bring her up, but he never seemed to remember by the time he finished mourning. Then he would blame me for starting the conversation and make me leave the apartment for as long as two hours so he could be alone and "regroup". Usually this happened at night when kids weren't supposed to be on the streets, so I would sit on the fire escape behind our building and look into the neighbors' windows. I liked watching families sitting together in front of the TV, or old couples rocking side by side and smoking their cigarettes. If dad kicked me out of the apartment early enough I could spy on people having dinner. I liked doing that most of all, watching people eat. It didn't make me hungry like it probably should have. It made me feel warm and excited to think one day that could be me eating a big steaming shepherd's pie.

Even three years after mom had left dad refused to admit why. He acted like it was because of a million different other things. His teeth were bad. Mom was embarrassed he hadn't gone to college. He didn't have a fancy suit-and-tie job. Mom didn't encourage dad's barrage of *why's* whenever he got into one of his drunken fits and decided to phone her to make things right, but she also never hung up until he was done. Experience had taught her that would result in him flipping out and smashing things around our apartment until either there was nothing left to smash or he was exhausted, and then he would cry on my shoulder until he passed out and drooled and squashed me under his drunk weight.

But back to Earl and the day before my thirteenth birthday. Dad actually phoned him that morning to come over and fix our toilet. It had been clogged for two days, and the smell could no longer be confined to the bathroom. It had become so strong no amount of Tabasco sauce on our eggs could cover up the aftertaste of shit.

"He's going to do it for cheap," dad said, as he pinched his nose and spooned eggs into his mouth. "Says I just gotta fill his tank with gas then we're square."

"Shouldn't he do it for free?" I couldn't eat so I shoved my eggs at dad. He reached over and spilled them onto his plate, eyeing me with that *waste not, want not* look poor people use to cover up the fact they're needy.

"Well I imagine so, Sammy, but you see I kind of…owe Earl some money already for, you know, house stuff and—"

The duct-taped rotary phone dad had picked up at Value Village clamored against the kitchen counter, and I flew to it. I was expecting mom to call and confirm she was going to pick me up the next day and take me to the shopping mall for my birthday. It was our yearly ritual. Since my birthday was right before Christmas she would take me to the big mall in Montreal on Saint Catherine Street, where there were larger-than-life mechanical reindeer at the center and a giant sleigh for kids to sit in. Santa Claus was there, too, but he always looked pissy and anyways I didn't believe in him. I just went for the reindeer. We usually went early in the morning before the mall stores were open so nobody could stop mom from lifting me onto the back of a reindeer. Signs all around warned people not to touch the reindeer because they were electrically operated, but mom said there was no risk in me being harmed from sitting on one for a few minutes. This year I wanted her to bring a camera so she could take my picture, and I could show my friends at school and they would finally believe me.

"Hi, mom! Tomorrow when you come and get me can you bring a cam—yeah, he's sitting at the table eating *diarrhea* eggs." I stuck my hand out with the receiver, but I refused to look at dad. He always got mom's attention first.

Dad took his usual forever to react, and I'm sure he could hear my internal time bomb ticking angrily. Finally he sighed the sigh only a divorced parent who feels he got the rotten end of the deal sighs and took the receiver.

"Why don't you go put incense and candles all around the coffee table like you like," he said loud enough so my mother could hear. "Me and *Earl* will do something fun with you today and *I'll* take you to the reindeer tomorrow."

I went to my bedroom instead. In reality, mom hadn't taken me to the mall for my birthday since she had left us. And actually maybe she never had and I had dreamed it up, like I had Earl the Wizard.

Fuck you fuck you fuck you ffffuck,
    fuck you fuck you fuck you ffffuck.
Whenever I was mad I sang "Twinkle Twinkle Little Star" but with my own lyrics. I liked the simple melody. I would flat-out yell the song

to the world from my bedroom window whenever I was the most upset I'd been in a long time, but this time I wanted to hear dad's end of the conversation with mom. It made me want to puke. His voice was all soft and cooey and he laughed for seconds at a time, which meant mom was charming him. Whenever she charmed him it was because she wanted something, because otherwise she was not a charming person. What she wanted now, of course, was to back out of her parental obligations to her daughter on her thirteenth birthday and, of course, I was not the one to ask permission from for this even though I was the one who would be most affected.

Fuck you fuck you fuck you ffffuck,
fuck you fuck you fuck you ffffuck!

I heard dad say, "Well yes, Marie, I do have things to say to you, and I think that since it's Christmas I should be able to say them so I can feel good for once." Right then I wished he would be seized with stomach pains from too much Tabasco sauce and shit all over the floor.

What did he have to feel so bad about? I was the one with an occasional mother and a loser dad who sniveled like a baby even though he was thirty years old. I stuck a hand in my mouth and bit until the skin on the back part broke. Just a little. Just enough to give me something else to worry about, like infecting myself with tetanus the way I had seen a guy do on the *Jerry Springer* show. I sat cross-legged on my bedroom floor and waited for the tetanus to set in. On TV, the guy had said it had been only a matter of seconds before he started to feel the lockjaw and insanity take over. It was a miracle he had survived. He had almost chewed his arm off, the tetanus made him so crazy. The audience was so taken with the guy's story that they donated money to the Springer Fund so he could accomplish his life dream: swimming with sharks. Jerry Springer ended the show by looking seriously into the camera and saying, "If somebody you love has tetanus, bring them to the nearest hospital immediately. You could help them accomplish a life dream." What if it was somebody you hated who had tetanus?

I got bored when the tetanus didn't set in, so I went to dad's room and turned on the TV. The *Maury* show, a total *Springer* rip-off, was on and a couple was breaking up in front of the world because the husband had cheated on the wife. I waited in suspense for the wife to come on set. I figured the guy sitting beside the husband was his brother, there to defend him as was customary on this kind of show, and it made me feel giddy. This could turn into something really ugly. But when Maury turned to the brother and asked, "Can you remember *when* your husband first started showing signs of infidelity?" all of a sudden I felt vulnerable and afraid. If there were people in this world who could trick you into thinking they were men when they were really women then what other kinds of people were there? Maybe it was better if not mom, not *anybody* paid any attention to my birthday this year. Maybe I should stay twelve and three hundred and sixty-four days forever.

According to Maury there were two ways to cheat on the person you loved. One, you could never ever plan to do it but then one day bump into the most terrific person you'd ever seen and become so obsessed with their terrificness the only way to deal with it was to orchestrate a situation where you both lost self-control and just went for it. But it would only happen that once because in reality the person wasn't so terrific, and it was just because your boyfriend or girlfriend had become old news to you. You'd realize after, though, that they knew about the little spot behind your knee and could tell when you'd had enough of one thing and were ready for another, and that, you'd realize with a touch of sadness, was something Mr. or Mrs. Terrific would never know.

That was how it was going to happen with Earl, I decided. He was going to see me for the first time and become obsessed with how terrific I was. He would see way past what my parents saw, and he would stroke my hair when we were alone and tell me I was perfect and he was so obsessed with me he couldn't stop thinking about me. I'd be secretly obsessed with him too but, since Earl was the same age as dad, I would have to tell him to wait until I was an adult, if he was so inclined. Earl's face would crumple, and he'd even get angry with me for asking him to stay single that long, but dad had taught me that men were weak about things like discipline so Earl would have to prove he wasn't before we could truly be together.

The other way to cheat was dull. Who would want to do it on purpose? Mom was always having affairs on her boyfriend, and she was forever crying about it. She had a whole other life to hide. Actually it was only a once-a-month thing with some guy who worked at a different branch of the same company as her, but it seemed like she spent all the days in between the rendezvous covering up her tracks. The guy didn't even buy her pretty things or take her anywhere special. That's what she told me once anyway, even though she denied it after the next time she saw him and said he treated her very nice. Like a lady. Ha ha. The wife on the *Maury* show said she wanted to be treated like a lady. Actually she demanded it on TV for the whole world to see, and I would damn well have done it if I were her husband because she was a pretty manly woman. I imagined she could pack some wild uppercuts and fart like a hot-air balloon. Suddenly I liked the man-wife on the *Maury* show. I liked her better than my mom. I was momentarily in love with her.

There was another way still to cheat on the person you loved. Actually more like *cheat* the person you loved and too boring a way for even a *Springer* rip-off show. It was the way that had made mom leave. It was Earl. Even when Earl was in prison for nine years dad devoted more time to him than me and mom combined. He hitchhiked all the way out to Kingston every weekend to stay in a roach motel just so he could visit Earl for an hour in a room filled with inmates on one side of a glass wall and stunned looking visitors on the other and black plastic phone receivers between them all.

On the weekends mom went to the Douglas I was sometimes completely alone if one of the neighbors couldn't look after me. That was when I was eight, and it only happened once actually because that time I set the apartment on fire when I forgot to shut the stove off after I boiled water for my morning coffee. The fire department came and the police came and then a social worker came, and she brought me to a foster home until she tracked my parents down and told them I could be taken away for good if they didn't smarten up.

Things improved for a while after. Dad stopped visiting Earl in Kingston, mom started making outpatient visits to the hospital, and we did family stuff together on weekends like have lunch at hot-dog diners and watch movies at the Dollar Cinema. But the first time dad mentioned Earl after the social worker event, mom flipped.

"I don't care if he's your goddamn brother! I feel like he's more important to you than we are!"

Whenever mom and dad fought about something that involved me in the slightest way, they used me like a weapon. This time, since mom had started the fight, she plucked me off the couch where I was sitting watching Saturday morning cartoons and hugged me in front of her like we were allies.

"Me and Sammy, we need you to be that interested in *us*!"

"I am, Marie, but Earl needs—"

"Fuck Earl! He doesn't need you, it's that *shit* you sneak in—"

Dad's hands went crashing onto the kitchen table, and he used words I had never heard until then.

"You fucking bitch keep your whoretrap shut!" He glanced quickly at me, and I felt like it was all my fault. Mom let go and shoved me towards my room.

"Go pack your stuff. We're leaving."

But I didn't want to leave. I liked our little apartment that was on top of a corner store that sold alcohol after 10 PM and single cigarettes to kids for twenty-five cents apiece. I had grown to feel comforted by the sounds of alley cats raping each other at night and mental patients from the Douglas wailing lonesome nonsense at 5 AM pill time. Plus I had adorned my bedroom walls with pages from the *Montreal Mirror*.

Pictures of music bands I didn't know except having them plastered on my walls excited me with the possibility of one day seeing them live. Plus they were nicer to look at than water-stained plasterboard and also the *Montreal Mirror* was free. I didn't want to leave because ever since the social worker had spoken to my parents, we had spent more time together and our apartment felt like a real home.

"I don't want to pack anything," I announced, putting my hands on my hips like I had seen a pretty blonde girl do on *All My Children* when she refused to give up her work office to a sleazy woman who was obviously sleeping with the boss.

Mom looked at me with a slightly shocked expression, but it quickly changed to anger and she said, "If you don't go right now and pack your things, Sammy Jennings, I will leave without you."

That was the first time anybody had ever threatened me. I didn't like it. Even if it was my mom and actually even more so because it was her who had done it first. She had violated my right to experience being threatened, the rush of fear that was supposed to come with it. The first time I was threatened was supposed to be at school in the bathroom or in the hallways when nobody was around, and I had to depend on myself to fight off the predator. I was supposed to feel validated by my response to a threat, not betrayed by the threat itself.

I looked at dad, he looked away. He always looked away when he was worried so I decided he was scared I would leave him for mom. That broke my heart.

"I said I don't want to pack anything." Then I marched to my room and slid under my box spring and traced my finger over the coils until I heard the front door open and close in that finalizing way mom had when she was serious.

After I had traced all the coils, I went into the kitchen to be with dad. We were quiet until long after the sun went down. We didn't even turn any lights on. The illogical streetlamp in the alley outside our apartment was all dad needed to make sure I actually was there with him. That's what it seemed like anyways because he looked startled and relieved each time we made eye contact.

Before I was obsessed with Earl I liked a schizophrenic named Gilles. That was when I was eight, after I set the apartment on fire and me, mom and dad started acting like a real family. Gilles was an inpatient at the Douglas Hospital, but he frequently left unannounced and returned a few days later with treasures. He called himself "Pirate" and claimed the world was gushing with treasures only he could identify. Everybody else was sinful and wasteful and threw out perfectly good things because they thought they deserved better.

Dad liked to taunt Gilles whenever we went to the hospital to get mom after her weekends there. He'd find Gilles sitting in the rec room and go up to him all innocently and ask, "So, my man, what did you find this time?"

Depending on Gilles's mood, he would sometimes boast about a cracked mirror with a *fleur-de-lis* pattern on the frame that could advise you about the next Quebec referendum. Other times he would hang his head and drool onto the children's book he was reading. Dad liked those times best. He would skim his hand over Gilles's greasy hair tufts and say, "Maybe next time you'll find a clock that can tell us when the next bus is coming so we can all get home on time. Ahhhh ha ha haaaa!" That would make Gilles whimper because he was terrified of buses. Then dad would slap him on the shoulder so hard he'd fall off his chair and whimper dumbly on the floor until the orderly came and collected him and gave him what dad called "happy pills". I was never too sure about dad's pill theory. Sure, they made Gilles stop whimpering, but they also made him stop altogether. His eyes would loll randomly in their cavities as if the only thing keeping them there was chance, and the rest of his face would lose its shape and resemble an undercooked pancake. I always had the urge to poke my finger into Gilles's cheek whenever he went catatonic. I had this fantasy it would feel like warm cookie dough. One time I lingered behind while dad went to find mom, and I put my nose up to Gilles's face. It was moist and rubbery and smelled like wet newspaper.

Once the doctor wanted to talk to my parents alone, so dad left me in the rec room with Gilles and a bunch of other crazy people and said all I had to do to keep them away was flash my bellybutton. He said crazy people were scared shitless of bellybuttons because it reminded them of the day they were born, and that was a bad day because they had been born crazy. So after dad made his usual fun of Gilles, who was in one of his down moods that day, I pulled up a plastic lawn chair beside him at the window overlooking a hedge garden. I had never spoken to Gilles before. I was pretty sure he hated me actually because I was the daughter of a man who made fun of him all the time. I sat beside Gilles like I was naturally supposed to be sitting beside him but, in truth, my legs felt like pieces of string. When Gilles all of a sudden asked me if I liked the hedges, I snapped my knees up under my chin and yelled, "What hedges?"

A few people in the room stopped playing their card games and knitting booties for their pretend children. The orderly sitting at the door to the rec room popped an eye over his newspaper, but I guess he was used to much worse than some scraggly girl scared by a mental patient.

Gilles was calm. He didn't even look at me when he talked. "I wonder how much they pay the gardener to trim them."

I felt like somehow I was supposed to know the answer. "Um—"

"Maybe when I'm better they'll let me trim the hedges," Gilles continued.

"But wouldn't you be gone from here then?" I mean, who on earth would want to come back to the Douglas to trim the hedges? Plus it was bad for the rehabilitation process. Whenever dad came home from an AA meeting he made me help him get everything out of the apartment that was in any way associated with his drinking. That was usually everything that wasn't a piece of furniture, but one time he made me throw out a TV set because he had watched an episode of *Cops* on it about an alcoholic who had led the police on a five-hour car chase.

"Oh, I'll never officially leave here," Gilles admitted, finally looking at me. He had these droopy eyes that were so sad they had no color. They were private school gray, and they looked soft. They reminded me of felt paper like the kind we used to glue macaroni faces onto in kindergarten.

"Who says?" I asked, acting like there was hope even though I had no idea what I was talking about. I was good at doing that, dad had once told me. He said it was a virtue to be able to make people think you knew a lot of things. They trusted you more quickly and would open up to you and tell you things that could spin your head. But I didn't want my head to spin. I felt like that was a cheap high, like mom said dad and his friends were always after. I wanted Gilles to feel like he could trust me. His eyes were so sad it made me feel depressed in the way a night without noise or the moon can make you feel depressed.

"I have a disease," Gilles whispered, leaning towards me. His breath smelled like old peanut butter. "But really it's a gift and that's why they'll never let me out of here. I bring back *treasures*, and the hospital needs my treasures to keep operating."

I was thunderstruck. Here dad had been making fun of this man with the sad eyes at the rec room window when, in fact, he was the reason there was a rec room at all! And next Gilles, sensing my excitement I guess, probed into his flannel housecoat and offered me a gift. I had no idea what it was except green and fluffy, like a ski hat pom-pom. Gilles dropped it into my hand and closed his hand around mine and whispered into my ear. I didn't catch all of what he said because the smell of old peanut butter got in the way, but it didn't matter. Gilles could have said, "I am going to kill you," and it would have sounded just as sweet. He was the first man ever, except dad, to give me a gift. A green ski hat pom-pom that I carried around in my pocket every day until one time

I forgot to remove it for the wash, and it dissolved in my jeans pocket and oozed green dye all down the right leg. The kids at school made fun of me when they saw my unintentional tie-dyed jeans, but they worshipped me when I told them about Pirate. Suddenly every kid wanted a green ski hat pom-pom to leave in their jeans for the wash.

The next time I went back to the hospital with dad I volunteered to stay in the rec room while he spent time with mom. I insisted he needed alone time with her. I skipped into the rec room with a haiku for Gilles secretly folded in the symbolic pocket of my tie-dyed jeans, but his chair by the window was empty. The orderly who seemed to live in the chair by the rec room door looked more bored than ever. He wasn't even reading a newspaper. He was rocking back and forth and staring at the wall like most of the mental patients did.

"Where's Gilles?" I asked.

The orderly gazed at me lazily and went back to staring at the wall.

"Pirate?" I pushed.

"Bled himself dry last night."

"Huh?" I didn't know what that meant exactly, but it involved the word *blood* so it couldn't be good. My face began to itch, and the feeling of little ants trickled down the insides of my legs.

"Finit. Kaput. Vacancy in the chair by the window," chanted the orderly, his interest in his environment suddenly renewing when two men in hospital gowns and IV's hooked to them started hissing at each other.

I didn't tell my parents about Gilles when they came to get me. I think mom already knew actually because, when dad asked where the pirate had sailed off to, she suggested we stop for pizza somewhere on the way home. Dad responded by pretending to drool all over himself like a mental patient at the mention of pizza. Some of the real patients giggled, and that seemed to satisfy him.

I had had my first experience of being in love at age eight, and neither of my parents had known a thing about it. To them I still lived in a world of stuffed animals and imaginary people. And they never thought to ask me in the years after Gilles how I was doing on the love front. They were too busy hating each other.

When Earl showed up I was watching *All My Children*. The pretty blonde had finally been forced out of her office by the boss's tramp. She talked to a co-worker as she packed, and the boss's tramp watched greedily from her own office.

"It's not fair!" exclaimed the blonde.

I loved the way she spoke. She made simple words sound urgent, like they were ripe with secrets. The co-worker looked enraptured as he watched the blonde organize her desk knick-knacks. The blonde glanced over her shoulder at the tramp watching from her office, and then cleared her desk with a defiant, elegant sweep of her arm. Her mascara ran in symmetrical streaks down her symmetrical cheeks, and I thought she looked beautiful in her state of upset. Every time she moved, the column of silver bangles on her forearm clinked like pennies being tossed into a shopping mall fountain with no water in it.

During the commercials I sat up on dad's bed and scrutinized myself in the dresser mirror. The dresser had belonged to his great-grandmother, and it was made of the heaviest materials imaginable. Once it had been made of pure pine, but now it was an ensemble of rusted steel and hardware store woods, because furniture passed on to dad never stayed in its original condition. He had moved a lot in the earlier years of his adult life and had each time refused to hire professionals. All a man needed, he claimed, was a best friend, a trailer, and a truck.

According to mom, dad always had his essential ingredients for a successful move except that Earl had back problems, Earl's truck stalled on roads that weren't perfectly flat, and Earl's trailer always unhitched from the truck five minutes into the trip. And so the dresser had made contact with the pavement at different speeds over the years, been pelted with hail the size of golf balls when dad got evicted from his first apartment one winter because he refused to pay rent until the downstairs tenants were kicked out for waking up at 6 AM on weekdays, and it had been rained on with God's biggest tears because it always rained when dad moved. But despite everything, the dresser mirror hadn't broken once, not even a crack. "The miracle mirror," dad called it whenever anybody asked how he had found such a perfect replacement.

I didn't think it was such a miracle on the afternoon before my thirteenth birthday. One thing about that mirror was it made you look ugly all the time. No amount of perfect lighting or clothes or hair gel or makeup could help. In fact the more you tried to pretty yourself, the uglier you looked. Maybe it was because I had just been watching a soap opera where everybody was unnaturally perfect, that was why I looked reprehensible that afternoon. Half the hair on my head was flat from lying on it while I watched TV, that same side of my face had large red pillow creases on it, and my favorite light blue jogging set with white racing stripes down the sides of the legs and arms looked more like pajamas than something I actually wore in public three times a week. It didn't help either that there was a large orange Kool-Aid stain down the front of the shirt.

I heard the entrance buzzer that had been wrongly placed on the wall outside my bedroom, which was right beside dad's bedroom, which was at the end of the hallway and far away from the front door. I heard dad jump to his feet like a dog that's been waiting all day for its owner to return home from work. I scurried to my feet, too, like the second dog of the house that has to be locked up in a cage all day because it might pee all over the place and chew table legs. This was it. I was finally going to meet Earl! My Wizard. My crush of nearly three years since Gilles had broken my heart and bled himself to death.

I leaned towards the dresser mirror and scowled. Something had to be done about my reprehensible state. When I was eight I could get away with some of the outfits my parents had made me wear. Actually it was mostly mom who had made me wear ridiculous things, like a bright pink velvet jumpsuit and frilly navy blouse and black patent Mary-Janes. After she left us, dad and I made a sort of silent agreement that I could dress however I liked as long as he didn't have to pay a lot of money for it. That was fine by me because I wasn't a clotheshorse, really. Every once in a while I'd fall completely in love with something and beg dad to get it for me, and then promise not to ask for something new until I wore it out, which was what I literally did a lot of the time. The light blue jogging set I had on wasn't quite worn out yet, but suddenly I panicked over the fact that it was one of the few coordinated outfits I owned. That was one thing dad and I agreed on happily insofar as my dress style. I liked the uniform look. "Minimalism," he called it. Just like him. We got along on that front very well actually. I was all about solid colors, two at a time maximum, and no flowers or polka dots or animals or logos. Dad's pet peeve was pinstripes. I secretly liked pinstripes, but they didn't make girls' clothes with pinstripes. I hoped Earl wore pinstripes.

"God-*dang*, David, ya look like ya just crawled out of a muffler, there!"

My body livened with little electrical sensations just listening to Earl's booming voice. Of course the walls in our apartment weren't very thick, so it didn't take much to be heard from one room to the next, but Earl's voice was ten times louder than anything I had ever heard. To me, it sounded like the voice of a larger-than-life man. A wizard. Dad laughed in that proud way he did whenever his friends came to visit and he felt like a worthy person, like how he laughed whenever mom called him a loser. Earl declared he had brought a two-four and some beer nuts and all that was missing was a good skin flick. I didn't know what "skin flick" meant, but it sounded mysterious, so I held my breath and waited for Earl to tell more. The whole time I was holding my breath, I was also running my fingers through my hair and patting the pillow creases from my face. There wasn't much I could do about my jogging suit, but if Earl was the kind of guy I hoped he was, then a little Kool-Aid wouldn't stand in the way.

I sat there on the bed for a long time, combing my hair and patting my cheek and being as quiet as I could so I could hear dad and Earl talk and open cans of beer and bags of beer nuts.

"No *sf*s tonight, Earl. It's Sammy's birthday tomorrow and Marie's got better things to do so I told Sammy we'd do a little something with her tonight instead."

"Well that don't mean we can't watch no *sf*s after she goes to bed, there."

"Quit it with your bloody *sf*s, man! That all you ever think about?"

"Just about."

They talked about other guy things until I realized there I was sitting all by myself in dad's room having not yet met Earl. I felt insulted, for I had thought Earl would have at least asked to say "Hi" to me by now, given we had never formally met. Finally dad came into the bedroom, but it wasn't for me, it was for pizza money.

"You like all-dressed, Sam?" He probably wouldn't have even noticed me if I hadn't cleared my throat in the official way I did, something he himself had taught me how to do when somebody's attention was required.

"Dad?"

"What, Baby?"

"Can I meet Earl now, please?"

Dad stopped in his tracks and turned to me with an expression akin to pity. "Of course, Sammy. You could have met him the second he came in."

I tossed a last glance at myself in the mirror and said, "I was waiting for you to tell me it was okay to be introduced."

Dad gave me a funny look, like I had just said the strangest thing, and then burst into laughter, the daddy kind of laughter that eventually made me smile and get over myself. "Hey, Earl! Don't you go ordering that pizza until I *introduce* you to my Baby Girl!"

Then suddenly Earl was standing under the bedroom doorframe, a bottle of Triple-X in one hand and our portable phone in the other.

"Earl," dad began with a great sweep of his arm, "this is my Baby Girl, Sammy."

Earl brought his hand to his forehead and tipped his hat, so to speak, then raised his beer bottle into the air and toasted.

"And Sammy, my sweet Baby Girl," dad continued, pulling my hand towards where Earl was standing, "this is my best friend and partner in crime, Earl."

Earl stepped into the bedroom and took my hand from dad's. I thought I was going to fall over the edge of the bed, he stretched my arm out so far. When Earl made actual contact with me, I thought my hand might slide right out of his because I was suddenly very sweaty. And not the good kind of sweaty. No, it was that chilly wetness your body produces when it knows there's something wrong about the given situation but your mind hasn't understood it yet. I didn't like having this feeling, because I had been in love with Earl for three years and now was the big moment, but I felt what I felt and that led to embarrassment and that led to me jumping off the bed and running into the bathroom where I slammed the door and stayed until after the pizza man delivered our supper.

I finally came out of the bathroom when my stomach started rumbling so loud Earl hollered from the living room that a small gremlin might be living in the toilet. Also, he hadn't yet fixed the toilet, so you can imagine how awful it smelled to be cooped up in a bathroom with no window or functioning air vent. I came into a pretty messy living room considering it had been clean only a few hours before, and not much had happened since except the arrival of a third person in our apartment plus some beer, beer nuts and now pizza. Still, the carton from the two-four had been torn up and thrown on the ground to soak up the mess from Earl's slushy boots, there were beer caps on the coffee table where my incense was supposed to be, and a slice of the all-dressed pizza had been converted into a stopper for our uneven, wobbly coffee table. As for dad and Earl, they sprawled on separate easy chairs and stared at the TV.

It took a while for my appetite to amount to anything after sitting in the bathroom stench for so long, so I went to my bedroom and retrieved Mr. Stripes, an old raggedy tiger dad had got me from the Salvation Army. I figured he could keep me company until I was hungry since dad and Earl had seemed to run out of conversational ideas and were satisfied with the hockey game that was on. Earl seemed to get a burst of energy right after I sat down, though, like a great big idea just popped into his fuzzed-out head.

"Hey now, that's a funny looking thing you've got there," he grinned, pointing at Mr. Stripes, who I had placed between my crossed legs.

"Got that dirty old thing for her when she was seven. Hasn't let go of it since."

"Da-*ad*!" He had never talked about Mr. Stripes like that before and, in fact, he had told me more than once that of all the stuffed animals he could have chosen for me that day, he knew Mr. Stripes was the right one. I wanted to say that out loud, but then I didn't want to share personal moments without dad's permission.

"Mr. Stripes is not dirty," I said, starting to feel testy. "He was like this when you got him for me, maybe even dirtier, but we washed him." Earl leaned over the arm of his easy chair and reached towards me. I closed my legs around Mr. Stripes and pretended to watch the hockey game.

"Ah, come on, Sammy Girl. Let's have a look at old Stripey, there." Earl batted at the air like a cat batting at yarn, but I didn't offer him Mr. Stripes. "Pleaaaase?"

"No." If Earl continued like this I was going to have no appetite at all, and because our fridge was empty I panicked a bit at the idea of maybe having to clean off the slice of pizza under the coffee table for later, since by then the rest of the pizza would be gone, and I was quite sure dad didn't have any more money to spend for the night.

Dad lifted a rubbery arm and told me to give Mr. Stripes to Earl.

I didn't want to. "What does he need to hold him for?"

Dad's arm hung in the air for a few seconds, and then he sat up and spoke to Earl as if I wasn't right there in the room with them. "Sorry, man, the toy *is* hers. She hasn't been that possessive over anything since…you know I don't think she ever was possessive over her toys." Then he teetered to his feet and announced he was making a run to the *dépanneur* for more beer. The two-four Earl had brought was done for.

I imagined what mom would have to say when I told her how dad had drunk more beer in one night than I had seen him do in months. Depending on her mood, maybe she would curse a bit and cup my face in her hands and apologize for having made the mistake of leaving me with "that *estie de* loser." Maybe I'd even get a new pair of mittens and a hot chocolate out of it. But more likely she would curse and then tell me she couldn't deal with that right now, she had bigger worries on her mind like her stupid affair's stupid plan to take her on a stupid cruise somewhere warm to prove that he loved her.

After dad left it was just me and Earl, and again Earl seemed to get another burst of energy. He rolled up to a sitting position and lit a cigarette.

"You don't think you're a bit old for stuffed animals, there?"

My common sense told me to ignore Earl and his big smelly ring of smoke, but he was dad's friend since forever and I didn't want to be a brat. So I told my common sense to shut up, dad would be back in ten minutes.

"Here."

Earl took Mr. Stripes from me and turned him around and around in one hand, whistling like he was looking at a brand new sports car or something. "Very nice, very nice indeed. And do you sleep with Mr. Stripes, little girl?"

Earl's question bothered me, the way he called me "little girl", so I reached for Mr. Stripes. "I do sometimes, just like everybody else in the world. And actually he makes a good extra pillow."

Earl raised his arm above his head, and the only way I would have been able to get Mr. Stripes from him would have been to stand up and jump in the air.

"Can I have my tiger back, please?"

"So he's not even a little stuffy to you, he's a *real tiger*," Earl purred, bringing Mr. Stripes right up to his face and squeezing until Mr. Stripes's plush insides started to spill out the small tear in his back.

"Stop!" Now I was on my feet and ready to charge at Earl if I had to. But the problem was I didn't want to go near him, this man I had imagined as something magical when in fact he was a smelly beer-drinking guy like all the others dad brought into the apartment.

Earl grinned at me like the ugly Cheshire cat.

I started to cry. "I want Mr. Stripes back."

"Say *please*."

"I did already!"

"No you didn't. You were quite rude there, like a spoiled little girl. Now say *please* and maybe, just maybe I'll give him back to you."

So I said please over and over and over, and then I started hopping from foot to foot as I said it, but Earl still didn't give Mr. Stripes back. He smiled and stuck a finger into the hole in Mr. Stripes's back and twirled him around the tip of his finger like the Harlem Globetrotters with their basketballs. I cried and cried and cried and got tears and snot all over my jogging suit and then finally dad came back and asked what the problem was and Earl said, "I think your *baby girl* there is pooped from all them soap operas she watched this afternoon."

"Dad, Earl won't—" But then Earl did. He threw Mr. Stripes at me in exchange for the beer dad handed him, and Mr. Stripes landed on the floor right in one of the puddles from Earl's boots, and then everything went back to normal. Dad told me to get ready for bed because it was clear I wasn't in a Birthday Girl mood, and then he settled into his easy chair and he and Earl were off onto another conversation and I became an old thought standing off to the side in the living room.

I lay in bed for the longest time trying to block out what Earl had done to Mr. Stripes. Every last thing he had said about Mr. Stripes upset me, and I was especially mad at myself for having let him do what he did for as long as he did. I could have stopped Earl at any time, but for some stupid reason I let him keep on calling Mr. Stripes a baby's toy, let him throw Mr. Stripes up in the air and land on the muddy, pizza-slime floor. Why had I done that? And why did I care, because Mr. Stripes was just a stupid toy anyway.

Usually Mr. Stripes slept in bed with me, right on my pillow, and that's how we started out that night, but then hearing dad and Earl get drunker and drunker and talk about all the things mom always used to yell about made me feel nervous and that, in turn, made me start to think of Mr. Stripes as a monster. I cried and shoved him under my bed, apologizing, but it just had to be that he stayed there until he didn't scare me anymore. And then I confessed to him that maybe he would stay there forever because I was, in fact, getting older and women didn't sleep with stuffed animals.

Even though I couldn't see him because he was under my bed, I knew exactly the look on Mr. Stripes's face as I told him about probable eventualities. I could see so clearly his shiny black eyes, all scratched up from his owner before me who had obviously dropped him on hard surfaces a lot. I could see Mr. Stripes's thread mouth, drooping down on the right side and disappearing on the left where the thread had frayed off just before it was supposed to turn up like a smile. I cried for Mr. Stripes, but I cried even harder for Earl, my not-wizard. My not-wizard had made me cry and probably knew I was still crying, and he was probably celebrating his victory with beer and beer nuts and skin flicks, for I had heard through the walls that dad had brought back a few with the new two-four.

You'd think all that crying would have made me tired, but it didn't. I needed to change the thoughts going through my head, so I jumped out of bed and gathered all my stuffed animals and hid them underneath. If Mr. Stripes had to suffer because of what I let Earl do to him, then all my other stuffed animals had to keep him company, and I had to suffer alone. I didn't deserve any comforting. There were so many stuffed animals under my bed I could feel them pressing against the bottom of my mattress, little bumps in the night that reminded me about monsters and bad feelings. Finally I got out of bed one more time and turned on the light and started to cram all my stuffed animals into the pretty ladybug valise dad had found leftover in an all-night diner he once worked at as part of a government employment plan.

"Sammy? What's going on in there?"

I guess I had been making more noise than I thought, crying a little too loud and sniffling like a baby, and if there was one thing dad was good about, it was seeing to my needs when I was upset. But there wasn't anything he could do for me this time unless he wanted to kick Earl out of the apartment, and I couldn't ask him to do that because then I'd be turning into mom, and dad had said so many times after she left that he would never live with another woman like her. I assumed that meant even me.

"I'm okay," I lied through my teeth. All noise outside my bedroom suddenly stopped, and I realized with a great big surge of panic that maybe Earl had heard me crying after all. I was mortified by the possibility. He had already laughed at me once for crying when he took Mr. Stripes away from me, and now he could laugh at me again for still being upset about it.

Earl spoke. "Hope you're not mad I laughed at you before, there. I wasn't laughing *at* you but *with* you. I mean you're almost a girl of thirteen now, too old for *stuffies*." Earl tapped his fingers on the outside of my bedroom door, and I ran over and threw my weight against it in case he was planning to come in. Dad said something in a low harsh voice, probably a reprimand to Earl for teasing me.

"I'm okay," I squeaked. "I'm just…it's a bit stuffy in here so I'm re-organizing some things." I heard dad tell Earl I got that trait from my mother, who was a pro at keeping things ordered, and then Earl tapped on my bedroom door once more and said goodnight.

Good, I thought, dad's informed Earl I am a person with capabilities. Good. I didn't want to wake the next morning, the first morning of my thirteenth year, and have the first thing I saw be Earl laughing at me with his eyes because he thought I was a baby. I, of course, hoped with all my heart he wouldn't be there in the morning, but I knew how beer took people over and made them sleep like the dead.

I went back to bed and lay on my back, counting the cracks in my ceiling and humming any old tune that popped into my head so I wouldn't have to hear anything of what was going on in the living room. It was hard to fall asleep without Mr. Stripes beside me and even though I rarely slept with my other stuffed animals, I found the emptiness of my bedroom produced a chilly feeling that I couldn't solve with more blankets. But obviously I fell asleep because next thing I knew I woke up hungry like I had predicted I would. It was late in the night by then, and dad and Earl were snoring away in the living room. I tiptoed out of my bedroom and prayed to God there was some leftover pizza, or at least some bread and peanut butter in the kitchen. As I had feared, the pizza was finished, but there were two stale slices of white bread and a diner packet of strawberry jam. Maybe the thing I regretted most at that moment, my first waking moment at age thirteen, was not that mom wasn't taking me to the mall in the morning to sit on the reindeer but that I wasn't going to have anything to eat, really, let alone anything special and birthday-oriented.

I sat at the kitchen table in the dark and ate my bread and jam. Outside was so black and quiet that if I turned on even the tiniest of lights in the kitchen, it would have seemed like the whole block had suddenly lit up. I heard a ruffling sound and thought maybe dad was awake. In a quiet, quiet voice I asked, "Is there anything else to eat?"

Dad didn't answer so I figured he was so drunk his mind wasn't able to connect voices to places, and he might start conversing with the stereo speaker or rubber plant in the living room instead. I crept into the living room, but it was so dark I decided to stay in one place because

I didn't want to step on any surprises, especially not Earl if he hadn't fallen asleep on his easy chair.

"Dad," I whispered, "I'm hungry. Is there anything at all in the house?"

No answer.

A black form moved to the far end of the living room, and then I heard a belt buckle being undone, a gargly, laughing moan, a zipper being lowered, and then the same sound that watering a plant makes.

"Daddy?"

Another moan, more plant watering, a zipper being zipped up, a belt buckle clinking, and then Earl's drunk weight flopping back onto his easy chair.

I could smell Earl's urine from where I stood, it was that acidic, and I knew the rubber plant would be poisoned and limp by morning if I didn't try to save it before then. But I couldn't do anything except stand there in the dark and listen to two men snore, and block my nose from the combination of odors, and feel sorry about Mr. Stripes all crammed into a valise, and wonder what I was going to eat, finally, during the actual daytime of my thirteenth birthday.

A Marmalade Cat for Jenny

We never left them dangling there for long, swaying back and forth between the fenceposts, little Jenny's skipping rope suspending them above the ground in scuffed pink neckties. Sometimes Jenny would spy on us then come running over with glossy red eyes, flailing her knobby arms in the air, crying for her skipping rope back. Then Mark would step in front of her with arms folded over his chest, the way the old man always did before he removed the belt from his pants one self-satisfied loop at a time, and Jenny would dig her bald heels into the dirt and spin homeward on a dime, threatening to tell Ma. She never did though 'cause she knew her neck was the perfect size for a little pink necktie, and she also knew Mark enjoyed just the thought of her in nothing but that. Jenny was smart for a nine-year-old.

So when she ran to us all wild-eyed and well-eyed that dusty Sunday morning in late summer, raw streaks of skin on her face swelling through a week's worth of no bathing, it was nothing unusual when Mark started to fold his arms over his chest.

"That one's still alive," I said, nodding to the last of three orange tufts dangling from the skipping rope. The poor thing gurgled and swatted its claws at the air.

Mark turned his head over his shoulder and launched a wad of spit the size of a half-dollar onto the creature's head. The spit landed on its good eye (Mark had melted the other shut with the brass Zippo the old man had given him for his seventeenth birthday that spring), and the kitten gasped. "Choke on *that*."

Jenny dug her heels into the dirt like usual, but she didn't turn back for home that time. Though her whole body vibrated with shakes, she willed herself in place and only her twitching toes peeking through Ma's sandals gave her worry away.

"Ma's bleeding," she told Mark, as if he would care. Our Ma wasn't his.

According to Mark he didn't have a Ma, but everybody knew different. The day she got bail was the day he never saw her again, and by then he hadn't seen her since he was five so he didn't care none when the court placed him with us. *It'll be nice living with the Dearths,* Mark told me the judge said to him. *The Dearths are a good family, and the Missus'll take good care of that growing boy's appetite.* Sure, Ma fed Mark good, and he liked to brag about it to Jenny telling her he could feed her good, too. But the old man had had her first and even though he didn't like the old man any more than a person likes to stick a lit match in his eye, Mark kept away from little Jenny.

"Ma's bleeding bad," Jenny pushed, leaning straight-legged towards Mark until her calves looked like two glue sticks about to snap backwards. When he just kept on standing there she turned to me with tears and prayer all over her face.

"Scott, please come home. Pa's in one of his ways again."

Mark reached back and yanked the skipping rope when the last marmalade started to yowl.

Jenny crouched down to look at the kitten and cried out when it made a raspy noise and kicked its hind legs at her. "Can I have him, Mark? Please? Please can you give him to me? Marmalade color is my favorite kind!"

"Go home," Mark ordered, yanking the rope again.

"Nobody ever lets me have nothing."

"Now."

With that Jenny let out a big huff and spun homeward so sharp she left one of Ma's sandals behind.

"Jenny's right, you know," I said, scuffing my boot on the ground. "She has no friends around here. A little girl shouldn't be lonely like that."

Mark's eyes followed Jenny until she disappeared into the trailer park. "She don't need friends. You see how girls her age dress around here? Bunch of little whores."

He glowered over his shoulder at the last kitten. The unforgiving sun had welted the dirt, blood and spit onto its face thicker than pie-crust, and the two others were starting to shrivel like day-old party balloons.

"Won't hurt her to have a cat," I persisted, taking a swig from the flask Mark handed me.

Mark poured the backwash from his flask onto the live kitten's head and made it yelp. "What Jenny needs is a dog. Something real ugly and mean to keep that filthy bastard in his place."

It was rare Mark showed concern for what the old man was doing to Jenny. Most often he accused her of lying about it, making up stories to win his attention. Then she'd start to blubber and follow him around the trailer with her rosary, swearing on every last bead she was telling the truth. One time Mark made like he believed her, and Jenny went to hug him, but then he snatched her rosary and smacked her across the face with it and told her the next time she lied like that a doctor would have to remove each and every bead from her stomach one by one with a rusty butcher's knife.

Mark yawned. "Garbage truck should be here by now."

"Bill says to burn them right away now," I reminded him, taking out a can of gasoline from my rucksack. "Says it reeks up his dump too much doing it there."

"Bill's a lazy son of a bitch. All he does is drink and fuck."

Mark had been real unhappy since we moved to Neverlee County. He had wanted to go to the city, but the old man didn't want to live somewhere where his social security officer could make him get a job, and Ma really wanted a trailer with awnings on the windows and found the perfect one in Neverlee. It was a small community, only twenty lots besides ours, and the neighbors were quiet except one guy whose pit bull bitch moaned and groaned so loud after he took her in at night, the old man sometimes called the sheriff. There wasn't much to do, especially during summer when school was out, but Ma enjoyed cooking and cleaning for the senior neighbors, and the old man made some pals at the tavern. Me and Mark found ourselves a job, if you could call it that, "keeping the community clean" by killing off strays. Kittens mostly, there seemed to be a new litter born every day, but sometimes there were pups and Mark liked dogs better so he went easier on them. He was always keeping an eye out for a good pup for Jenny even though he knew she wanted a kitten. And that last one hanging on the rope, well, it was kind of cute despite its burnt eye and all.

"It's Jenny's birthday tomorrow," I said.

Mark leaned his leg against the fencepost and rolled two cigarettes. He lit one for me, the other for himself, and then he held the old man's Zippo under the marmalade's backside.

"I thought about giving this one to her," he drawled proudly, admiring the flame as it grew and crept up the tiny orange tail. "Then she come over and seen it so it wouldn't be a surprise tomorrow, now would it?"

"Guess not," I answered, feeling a bit sad for the squealing animal.

Once the squealing became too much for even Mark, he untied the kittens from the fencepost and kicked them into a pile to pour gasoline all over them. The three together didn't amount to the size of a full-grown cat, but they smelled as bad as any burning thing. After that, we packed our stuff and headed across the field for home to see what was wrong with Ma.

"What about Jenny's skipping rope?" I asked.

"She can get it herself."

"It's no good now."

"So?"

"So she don't have another, and she likes to play rope after mass."

"Pa'll take care of her."

It was nearing high noon, and the sun was so heavy and sticky everything around us looked flattened to the ground with a layer of see-thru glue. The cracking sounds under our work boots confirmed we had been in a drought all summer although the trailer park rippled and shimmered ahead like a freshly watered plant. About a quarter-mile away from home, we came to a pile of deflated truck tires and crushed beer cans and sitting right on top was old Millie, one of the neighbor's cats that was having a new litter every month it seemed. She gazed up at us with lazy yellow eyes and stretched a front paw in the air as if to say, *Why y'all lookin' so sour?*

"Whore." Mark walked past Millie so close he knocked one of the tires sideways and she slid off her fort. She landed in the grass heavy like the babies inside her were rocks instead, and suddenly she didn't look so self-satisfied anymore. I watched the old girl work at standing up, spreading out her four limbs to steady herself, and called to Mark when she let out that unmistakable pre-birthing groan.

"She's gonna have them tonight."

"So?"

"We could give one to Jenny."

Mark stopped and turned to watch Millie, who had finally assembled herself into a standing position and was waddling over to me with that combination look of fear and expectation all females get before they birth. Ma had looked that way before she gave birth to Jenny. Everybody else had been excited about my little sister's coming into this world, and I remember not being able to understand why Ma was preparing for the event like a person prepares for a funeral.

Mark made like he was going to come over and inspect Millie, but in the end he said, "If it means so much to you then bring the cat back and hide it under the trailer," and continued home.

I thought hard about bringing Millie home and keeping her until she birthed, but if she had her babies when the old man was around then not a one of them, not even little Jenny's kitten, would live to suckle its first milk. Truth was I didn't like the old man and what he was doing to Jenny any more than Mark did, but I couldn't stand against him the way Mark did.

Most of the neighbors were getting ready for afternoon mass as me and Mark walked between the rows of trailers to ours at the back of the park. The church was just past the tavern, and everybody walked there together chit-chatting the whole way about anybody who hadn't come along. Me and Mark would go with them, but the old man always took Ma and Jenny through the backroads. Didn't want them subjected to foulness, he said, and he certainly didn't want Jenny mixing with kids who spoke with mouths dirtier than their folks'.

One time before we left for mass, Mark pretended to be the old man making the sign of the cross then choking on the wafer 'cause his sins were too great, and Jenny joined in laughing her little girl's laugh. I kept an ear out for the old man as I sat on the trailer step watching them 'cause I knew this was not something he would find funny. Mark didn't care and Jenny, why she was only seven at the time and all she saw was Mark having fun and that meant something to her. When the old man came outside, Mark up and walked off to join the neighbors and left poor Jenny none the smarter for it, dancing around in mock convulsions singing *Praise the Lord!* I had a mind to say something, but the old man saw me thinking it so I just sat there until Jenny's screeching apologies disappeared after the old man and her hit the backroads. There was no point in mentioning anything by the time I caught up to Mark.

"Hear the Missus ain't doing so good," an old lady said as we neared her trailer. I had seen her around often enough, and she had spent dinner with us one night after her husband died, but other than that I didn't know who she was. Ma knew everybody in the park 'cause of her cooking and cleaning, and it always made me uncomfortable when people talked to me like they knew me too.

"She's fine," I answered, stopping at the old lady's step when she raised a wrinkled hand. Her fingers were long and curled, with knuckles that looked like Boy Scout knots, and fingernails painted the color of tea that's been left to sit too long.

"You're a good son, Scott," she croaked from underneath her floppy Sunday church hat. "You go and spend the day with your Ma while the rest of us pray for her."

"I will," I assured the old lady, who rolled her head back with a drooping, toothless smile.

Mark had continued on ahead and was pulling off his work boots by the time I reached our trailer.

It sounded like there was a small party going on inside. I leaned against the puckered aluminum side to remove my boots and heard Jenny whimper like a dog that's been starved for weeks and would be happy just to lick a bone. Inside, our little trailer was even littler with three ladies dressed all proper and a fat man holding Jenny on his lap, all of them sitting outside Ma's bedroom. Me and Mark watched Jenny bury her face in the fat man's greasy beard, watched the three ladies watch us, then Mark asked, "What's going on?"

"Oh, *honey*," one of the ladies wailed, holding her hand out.

Mark folded his arms over his chest and looked towards Ma's bedroom. "I said what's going on?"

Mark was a handsome boy in those days. Nobody believed he was just seventeen especially when they learned I was too. See, he was near six-foot-two and the sun had done him well. His eyes looked like crystals against his dark skin, so clear and so blue and green all at once you never knew which color they were. Even though Mark was still in grade eight he spoke with the coarse voice of a man who'd seen many things. People never asked if me and him were brothers 'cause they knew we weren't, but I knew the neighbors chit-chatted about us on those Sunday church walks we didn't attend. About how lanky Scott wasn't a man like Mark, couldn't stand up to the old man, couldn't take a smack in the jaw, couldn't protect Jenny. Poor little Jenny with her cotton-candy pigtails and chocolate eyes, sweet the way the old man liked.

"Your Ma's resting now, honey," one of the other ladies informed Mark. Her eyelids sagged with bright blue shadow, and her lashes looked like they'd been dipped in tar. She batted them at Mark the way most ladies did, especially on Sundays when they felt holy and attractive, but he paid no attention. He didn't have eyes for anybody but Jenny.

Mark glared at the gathering outside Ma's bedroom for a while longer then left without another word, slamming the screen door behind him so hard it jammed on the inside of the doorframe.

"Scott, good boy," the first lady crooned, patting her meaty thigh for me to come closer.

Jenny peeked up from under the fat man's beard, her eyes all pink and warning me something was very wrong with Ma. This was confirmed when the lady dropped her voice.

"Seems your Ma was *expecting* and there were some *complications.*"

"No she wasn't, no there wasn't." Though truth was I really had no idea.

"When your Pa found this out this morning," the lady continued, "he went down to the tavern looking for the man that done it."

"You stop this right now, ma'am." Maybe I hadn't known Ma was expecting, but I was one hundred percent sure she hadn't been with another man. If there was something I did know, Ma wasn't with the old man 'cause she had no choice. Him, me and Jenny, even Mark, we were her choice.

"Scott, please be kind and let me finish."

"Not unless you got something real to say."

"I do! When your Pa couldn't find the guilty he came home and got into a bit of a fight with your Ma. She was already having stomach pains this morning so this is how she knew she was expecting, and then with the fighting and all, and you know how your Pa can have a rough hand sometimes. So it was an accident you see, and now your Ma's just resting up."

Jenny started to sob, and the two other ladies dabbed their eyes. The fat man sat there all content, keeping Jenny in place by sliding his oily fingers around the flash of skin between her T-shirt and shorts.

I felt sick looking at the heap of soggy paper towels on the kitchen table, the blood that had spilled between the cracks on the floor reminding me of one time as a kid I knocked Ma's fresh-made strawberry jam on the floor to get the old man's attention away from her.

The lady lowered her head and reached over to pat Jenny's leg. Jenny tucked her leg tight into her stomach, and the fat man tightened his hold on her in case she might want to wriggle off his lap.

I forced my upset back down my throat. "Everybody has to leave. Now."

But it wasn't me who made it happen, it was the old man yelling into the trailer so loud that like magic everybody jumped to their feet and scattered quick and quiet as church mice.

Jenny ran to her bedroom and slammed the door even though the old man had just ordered her to get dressed for mass. "No!" she screamed, pounding her cup-sized fists on the wall. "Ma's hurt so I'm staying."

The old man must have gone right to her window and reminded her about consequences, 'cause suddenly Jenny walked out of her bedroom all obedient and went to the bathroom to wash up. I was still standing in the hallway about as useful as a blind person without his cane until I thought of something to make her happy.

"Saw old Millie before. She's gonna have babies soon, and we were thinking of getting you one, a little marmalade like you want."

"Millie ain't gonna have marmalade babies," Jenny mumbled. "She's a black cat."

"So?" I chuckled, feeling like I was talking to a miniature adult. "Maybe the daddy's orange."

"Don't matter, Scott. Takes two marmalade cats to make a marmalade kitten."

Jenny patted her face dry and went into Ma's bedroom, closing the door firm behind her. She was in there a long time it felt like, and when I tried to go in she leaned against the door and told me to stay put.

"Pa says Ma has some ribbons I can put in my hair." A few minutes later Jenny slipped out with pigtails tied in pink ribbons, a matching imitation pearl necklace dangling down her neck. "Scott," she said, as she rummaged through a box of used clothes a neighbor had given her as an early birthday present.

"Yeah?"

Jenny didn't answer until she had dug out a pair of black patent Mary Janes that fit her almost perfect.

"After Pa and me leave, you and Mark should call Bill."

"Did you see the fight?"

"Pa's been drinking so much he don't even remember having affections with Ma. By the time she made him remember, he'd kicked the baby right out of her."

After Jenny left the trailer I opened Ma's bedroom door and peered in. Even though Bill wasn't the right person to call, Jenny was a smart nine-year-old for having kept the secret until after everybody left.

Wherever Mark went after he left that afternoon, he didn't come back until dark so I had to make the call myself. The neighbors who hadn't gone to mass all kept to themselves when the ambulance flashed its silent emergency lights as it pulled into the park, but they did a poor job of sitting on their front steps pretending not to be watching what was going on. The EMTs didn't ask me many questions, but they did insist the old man pay the service fee from his next social security check.

"Yes, sir," I answered with the eyes down of a person who knows he can't see such a promise through.

"And you're sure this was an accident, right?" one of the EMTs pretty much concluded, leaning away from the screen door like the old man was going to come barging through any second.

"Yes, sir," I agreed, in reality more worried about cleaning up the kitchen mess before anybody else stopped over.

"Well I'm sure Buster's gonna miss Lily. She was just twelve when you were born, you know."

"I know. We're gonna miss her."

But as the EMTs covered Ma and lifted her thin, hard body onto the stretcher I felt more sad for little Jenny. She wouldn't have anybody to run home to anymore.

"Pa, stop! That hurts!"

Jenny's scream was so loud that night I thought I was dreaming. I had only heard a scream like that once before and it had been a howl, the howl of a rabbit Mark caught with his bare hands when it tried to steal from Ma's garden. That was how me and him got our job "keeping the community clean", though it was only Mark's skills that were needed really. He was quick as a jackal while I just ended up his partner 'cause the old man had a long history with Bill and Bill wanted to do right by him. In the end we made for a good team with my keen abilities to spot strays, though sometimes I pretended not to see them, especially if I knew they belonged to anyone in the community. To Mark they were all the same, but I had my standards.

"Pa, please!"

Jenny's cries sounded like they had been stuffed inside a tin can, our bathroom was that small. The bath water started running and I heard the old man mutter something, whatever it was bringing Jenny's volume down to a scratch no louder than a record player's.

"…Pa …no …"

Mark sat up on his cot. "Shit. Wife ain't dead and gone one full day and he's poking his filthy fingers around."

"We should stay in here," I tried, my breath catching in my chest when I heard the old man's belt buckle clank against the bathtub. "You remember what happened last time."

Mark snapped out of bed and jammed his legs into his pants. Even in the dark I could see how black his eyes were, the color of retribution, and I knew there wasn't anything I could say to stop him. "You can stay here, you goddamn coward, but this is the last time that bastard's going near your sister."

Jenny howled again, and I swear I felt Mark shudder. I never saw him move so fast when the old man started to yell. All of a sudden there was pure noise. Things crashing, water splashing, voices hollering, I couldn't make out what was what. I sat there like a deer in headlights the whole time—seconds, minutes, I really can't say—then next thing I knew Mark turned on the bedroom light with Jenny in his arms. She was dripping wet from top to bottom, naked and shivering like Millie's kittens probably were if they'd been born yet.

Me and Jenny stared at each other, and it wasn't until that point in our lives I noticed how much she looked like the photographs of Ma from when she was young. Her eyes were wide and scared, but her face was unreadable just like Ma's had always been after the old man and her got into a fight. And even though her teeth were banging against each other hard as hammers, Jenny's lips were sealed so tight it looked like she was trapping a scream powerful enough to blow the roof off our trailer.

Mark was shaking too, and his hands were rinsed in blood, but otherwise he spoke with the voice of a man who knew he had been fair in his dealings.

"Get her dried and dressed," he told me, lowering Jenny onto my cot so tenderly she blushed.

"It's okay, Baby," he rasped, the drops of water on his face tricking me into thinking they were tears. "He ain't ever gonna hurt you again, but you and Scott have got to leave now, hear?"

"For how long?" whimpered Jenny, flinching when I started to dry her with my bed sheet.

"Am I hurting you?" I asked, even though I knew the truth. I was the only man in our family who never had, physically anyway.

"No, Scott. Mark, where are we supposed to go?"

Jenny kept flinching as I helped her into one of my T-shirts and tied her hair in a ponytail, and she kept staring up at Mark until he gave her the answer we all already knew.

"Go with Scott and knock on somebody's door, maybe one of them ladies from this aft. Say you need a place to stay until morning then Scott's gonna take care of you. Okay, Baby?"

Even though Mark was speaking to Jenny his eyes were fixed on me, and I could hear the undertone of threat in his voice. *You take care of her or you're next,* it was saying to me. So after we were dressed I took little Jenny's hand and we left the trailer. Left Mark behind to find me and Jenny a place to stay until the sheriff came and arrested him, until the ambulance came and took the old man's body to the hospital to join Ma's, until the court decided what would happen to me and my baby sister next.

"Jenny," Mark called through the screen door when we weren't even a few feet away.

"Yes?" Jenny spun around, the prayer for possibility so heavy in her voice I thought I saw Mark's hands come together behind his back.

"Happy birthday."

Everything happened pretty quick the next morning. The sheriff came and got Mark after he phoned and turned himself in, and then a car was sent for me and Jenny a while later. We had spent the night with the Mandys, a couple that claimed to have known Ma very well. Mrs. Mandy raved about the lovely corn muffins Ma used to bake for Sunday mass and even had the nerve to ask if I knew the recipe.

"That was her recipe," I answered, feeling insulted by Mrs. Mandy's talking about muffins while the lights flashed outside mine and Jenny's trailer and the sheriff came out with Mark, his hands cuffed behind his back. Mrs. Mandy caught on 'cause she suddenly changed the subject and invited Jenny to have a peek at her dress-up jewelry in case she wanted to take any with her.

"Take any with her where?" I snapped, a littler harsher than I had meant. It's just I was real tired having stayed up all night comforting Jenny, who didn't shed her last tear until sunrise.

"Well with your parents gone they'll probably place you somewhere and probably not together."

Just the mention sent Jenny into a new stampede of tears.

"We ain't going to no foster homes," I said with certainty, though in truth just the mention made me want to cry, too.

Mrs. Mandy's pancake batter face bloated with suspicion. "You're not thinking of running away with her, are you?"

I swigged my last mouthful of black coffee and slammed the mug on the table. "I'm eighteen soon, and I'll take care of Jenny. Law says at eighteen a person under special circumstances can. The trailer ain't a big expense if I quit school and get real hours from Bill, so I'll inform the court me and Jenny are staying together."

Mrs. Mandy shook her head like I was talking nonsense, but Mr. Mandy, who had been sitting at the table all quiet with his morning paper and chewing tobacco, peered over the *Neverlee Daily* and sided with me.

"Nothing wrong with a boy who wants to take care of his family," he said to his wife, whose eyes bounced out of their sockets. "That Buck kid managed okay with his sister."

"They didn't have the same kinds of *problems*," Mrs. Mandy sputtered all self-important.

"And just what kinds of *problems* do you mean?" I challenged, dropping my elbows on the table and leaning towards her. "Do you mean the kind like we're dirt poor like everybody else around here? Or do you mean the kind people like me and Jenny are sure to have 'cause of the old man?"

Mrs. Mandy's whole fat face jiggled like it had been slapped. "No need to get sharp, Scott. I was just saying."

"And I'm saying to you, Missus Mandy, none of it has made me the worse. And little Jenny, why little Jenny here's tough as nails."

When I looked over at Jenny, she was giving me that tulip of a smile I'd seen her give Mark so many times. "Yeah, me and Scott are tough as nails."

It took some negotiating the judge of course, before he banged his gavel and declared me a capable person to care for my baby sister, and it didn't come without rules. First I had to get a real job, not the killing stray animals kind, and the pay had to be more than the old man's social security had been. I had one week to do this.

The judge was asking the impossible on purpose (even though the law was there, I could see plain as day he wasn't happy about it in my case), so wasn't it my luck a construction company opened that summer just past the tavern and the church and was looking for roofers. The foreman snickered when he first saw me, said no way a scrap of a boy like me could hold two shingles together, but after I spent a full twelve-hour day out there under the unforgiving sun with men twice my size, he took me to the tavern and bought me a draft.

So the judge gave in but not without extra rules. Every Friday a lady named Debbie, who said she had cases like me and Jenny all over Neverlee, came to check up on things. Things like how clean the trailer was, how much food was in the kitchen and how healthy it was for a growing girl, what little Jenny wore, signs of alcohol around the place, did we still go to church. All this was recorded for a weekly report to the judge. That wasn't the biggest hassle though, 'cause me and Jenny lived clean, and the roofing job paid me good for my long days. The biggest hassle was the stuff that had to be taken care of between Fridays, the stuff not on Debbie's checklist but that I knew was being watched too.

For example, once summer ended and Jenny went back to school, somewhere in between my waking up, twelve-hour shift and going back to bed, I had to get her lunch ready for the next day, which meant needing time to buy lunch food in the first place. When Jenny needed help with her homework it didn't matter if I was tired, 'cause she was the priority. There was keeping an eye out for who Jenny spent time with after school, and that was almost impossible since I usually got home after dark. Then again Jenny wasn't interested in playing with other kids and Mrs. Mandy, mealy-mouthed Mrs. Mandy, kept her, feeding her and everything, on the days I worked late.

"Missus Mandy asked about Mark today," Jenny told me one night at supper, about a half-year after Mark had turned himself in for the old man's death.

Though nobody dared to say it out loud, everybody knew Mark had made up his mind that night, and it would always be in his nature to make up his mind about a person like that again. *First degree manslaughter!* one juror had railed. *Self-defense!* another had insisted. In the end the judge took pity on Mark's life circumstances and sentenced him to a locked rehabilitation facility until he turned twenty-one. Mark didn't argue none. Even when little Jenny started to bawl as the court officers cuffed his hands and feet and led him to the van, he kept a solid back. Every man watching him leave that day dropped his head in shame 'cause he couldn't stand the way Mark did.

"What'd Missus Mandy wanna know?"

"How Mark's doing, and when I told her I didn't know she asked me how come, 'cause he's like our brother."

I had been dreading this conversation from the beginning, not knowing how it would start, and knowing Mrs. Mandy had started it angered me. But in all my time dreading and even obsessing over it, I hadn't taken just one second to plan what I was going to say when the conversation actually happened.

"So how come we ain't heard from Mark?" Jenny pressed, the fine baby hairs on her arms lifting goosebumps all over her skin.

Everybody had tried to assure me the reason Jenny wasn't much interested in playing with other kids was they all had Ma's and Pa's to go home to and she didn't want to be reminded of that just yet, but I knew it was 'cause she missed Mark. Oh, the people made sense in their logic 'cause Jenny told me sometimes she missed our parents, but in the way she never told me she missed Mark, too, I knew that she did. And even though he had been hard with her, enjoying making her cry even, I was sure Mark missed her something mean. Having grown up seeing the old man wear Ma down to her death with his yelling and beating and drinking though, I had learned some kinds of love were dangerous, and I didn't want Jenny to have to find out the way Ma had.

"Mark can't talk to people outside the facility, Baby. It's like jail in there, all those guys living in four-by-four rooms with doors that lock from the outside and no windows to let the sun in."

"But we're family, Scott. Mister Mandy told me when Buck was separated from his sister he still got to talk to her."

"They were real family."

"Maybe you think Mark ain't real family," Jenny spat, slamming her fork onto her plate so loud I got potatoes stuck in my throat, "but all you ever do is *think*." Then she pushed her chair back and scampered to her room like a wounded animal that's more aware of the fact it's been wounded in front of another pair of eyes than the fact it's actually wounded.

Life went on like that for the next two-and-a-half years, me working my twelve-hour days putting a roof over Neverlee's first housing project, Jenny going to school then staying with the Mandys until I got home. On the summer of her eleventh birthday, Jenny asked me to register her in a babysitting course going on at the church. It's not that I didn't want her to learn those skills, but there was no way for me to walk her to and from the church every day with my work schedule, Mrs. Mandy was getting fatter by the month so she was no good to count on, and there were no other proper kids taking the course. I had just been promoted to supervisor though, and that meant better pay, so I made an offer to Jenny.

"What about going to camp?" I asked one afternoon after I came home early 'cause the sun had baked right through the roof I was working on.

"What kind of camp?"

"I was thinking a nice Christian camp. Saw a sign for one at the church when I went to see about your babysitting course."

"Oh. I don't care for church anymore, Scott." Jenny's voice was as thin as she was slight, and her lids were slipping down fast over her eyes.

"You been sleeping a lot lately," I said, changing the subject with a concern I was proud to be feeling 'cause it meant I was doing my job as good as any parent. "Do you wanna see a doctor?"

"No."

"I can afford it now so don't let that trouble you."

"No thanks, Scott. I'm just bleeding like girls do when they become women is all."

I wanted to respond and I was angry at myself for not having anything at all to say, but the only time I'd seen a woman bleed had been after the old man had his way with Ma and I knew this was not the same situation.

"Are there girls where Mark is?" Jenny asked.

I just sat there all dumb and blank. "Girls?"

"Yeah."

"Well, it's not so usual for girls to do the same bad things boys do, but I imagine there's a place for them too."

"I mean living with Mark. Are there girls there he can see every day?"

Even though me and Jenny had been facing each other the whole conversation, I suppose I wasn't really looking at her more than enough to notice she was near falling asleep. But her question about Mark living with girls caught me so off guard that I really looked at her, and that's when I saw a flush in her cheeks that little girls aren't supposed to have. And when Jenny asked me again if Mark lived with girls, the humidity in her voice made me understand what she had meant by just bleeding like a woman was all.

Mark was let go from the facility one morning in early spring just before his twenty-first birthday. Jenny was asleep when he phoned the night before with the news.

"You're talking kind of funny," he snickered, in a way that made me feel cold. "Got sandpaper on your tongue?"

"No," I whispered, "I don't wanna wake Jenny up."

"I'm sure she'd love to talk to me."

I said nothing so Mark changed the subject. "Making good money on the job?"

"Sure, but Jenny's starting high school in the fall so there'll be new expenses."

"No big deal," Mark drawled. "I'm coming home soon and I'll be working too, so there'll be lots of money."

My ears started to burn at Mark's talk of returning home, though I had always known the day would come. He didn't have anywhere else to go. His three years in the facility had been restricted so any friends he had made were from the inside, and from the stories he had told me they weren't guys anybody would want to know on the outside. Mark had made good use of his time in lockup, getting his high school diploma and learning mechanics. That was more than I could say for myself, even though my roofing job was secure and word was I would be getting another promotion soon. I felt what I had always thought of as my respect for Mark turn into flat-out jealousy.

"Lots happened since you left. You can't just come back and take over. Besides, who do you think'll hire you? Bill's dead from cancer, and trapping strays is a job for kids."

"I was thinking you could set me up in the projects, maybe as a welder or something."

Of course Mark was thinking that, and of course he knew even if I made like there was no room, the foreman would snatch him up in a second. The foreman was always looking for certified men. Even though I'd been promoted to supervisor 'cause of my natural ability to oversee things, the guy who took my old job had certified skills and was always one step behind whatever position I stood in line for next.

"You want a job, Mark, you talk to the foreman."

With that me and Mark hung up and I went to bed, staring at the ceiling for hours and feeling like little pins were nicking my sides every time I heard Jenny moan from the other side of the wall.

I don't know what exactly I was expecting to see when I came back from work the next night, whether it was Mark sitting at the kitchen table tearing into a thick red steak, or an empty trailer 'cause he was at the tavern welcoming himself home. Or maybe he had decided not to come home at all. Well it was none of that, but what it was seems to me now like the beginning of the end.

"If it ain't the old bricklayer's son!" Mark boomed as I stopped outside the trailer to take my work boots off. "Build any sandcastles today?"

Jenny was sitting beside Mark on the couch, her math book open on her lap and the only thing between his brawny hands and her.

"Scott!" she exclaimed, jumping up to come show me a page scribbled with equations I barely remembered doing before I'd left school. "Mark says he's gonna help me with my homework since you work so late. Says he can make me an A-student in no time!"

Oh how little Jenny's eyes were bright with happiness. Her cheeks swelled with smiles, and she pranced around me on spindly legs like a colt that's figured out how to keep up with its momma. Even Mark looked content as I watched his eyes follow her, content like on those rare occasions the old man had done something nice for Ma, and she went on thanking him for hours after the rest of us went to bed. As much as I tried to fight it a feeling of relief started to warm me, and I sat down at the kitchen table, Jenny's giggles and squeals rocking me into a sort of trance.

Mark slept in the living room that night out of a common decency he had never lacked, I admit. Jenny went to sleep in her bedroom, but I could hear the desire racing through those little veins of hers. That of course kept me up all night with one ear cocked for the sound of her eager feet padding to the living room, but she had always had a sense of decency about her, too.

The next morning Mark got up first and cooked us bacon and eggs shining in grease. When Jenny started for a second helping, he tapped her hand and said since she was a woman now she had to watch what she ate. If it had been me doing that Jenny would have curled her lip and said I wasn't her Pa. With Mark, her mouth twitched and her eyes grew muddy, but she pulled her hand back and sipped all tame-like on the orange juice he poured for her.

"I'll speak to the foreman about getting you on board," I said in my best effort to sound sincere. In reality I was doing it for Jenny, 'cause the foreman had offered me a six-week job in Eshewall City and I wanted to make sure she was taken care of while I was gone. I should have been worried about bigger things for her at the time, but then again it didn't take a genius to see Mark's return had permanently changed the order in our trailer.

"Spoke to him already," Mark bragged. "Told me you was leaving and Jenny would need providing so he's starting me at twelve dollars the hour."

Twelve dollars the hour. That was high starting pay for a welder all right. That was what I was getting as supervisor.

"I ain't leaving for good, Mark. Just six weeks."

"Don't matter," Mark drawled, winking at Jenny. "Foreman says there'll be other contracts coming up, and he wants you to head the crews."

"I'll refuse. I'm just taking this one 'cause it pays high."

"What about when you come back?"

"What about when I come back?"

"Your supervisor position's already been filled by somebody else, and I can't support *three* on twelve dollars the hour."

The whole time me and Mark were discussing the situation, little Jenny sipped her orange juice like we were talking about what was going to be for supper that night. Every so often she'd peek up at Mark and he'd wink at her, but whenever I tried to make contact she acted like she didn't notice.

"Jenny, Baby," I tried, having to lay my head sideways on the table to meet her eyes. "You know I ain't going for good, right?"

"Sure," she said, leaving the table to get ready for school.

Me and Mark sat across from each other like we used to when we were boys, only we were men now. And even though I was still scrawny and lanky compared to Mark, the past three years had taught me a lot.

"I've been saving every extra penny from work, Mark. I'm going to get us a nice little bungalow."

"Us?"

"Me and Jenny, in Eshewall if the city's nice. Don't want her doing school here any longer than she has to. Girls her age are out fooling around already."

"Does Jenny know? Last thing I heard from her she's looking forward to having a little party here first week of school."

"She can do that in Eshewall."

I had a mind to keep the conversation going until Mark got fed up and told me to just take Jenny and have a nice life in Eshewall, then I realized two things. One, Jenny was only turning thirteen that summer so she had no say and two, I was twenty-one soon so I could take her anywhere I saw fit. Once I turned twenty-one, no more Friday visits from Debbie, no more living under everybody else's surveillance on the days in between, no more Neverlee County. As if Mark could read my thoughts like a billboard sign on the side of the highway he leaned back in his chair and dug into his pocket.

"Here," he said, tossing a scrap of newspaper across the table. "This is what I'm planning to give Jenny to show her how much I've missed her, so you can see why she might rather stay here."

I unfolded the damp paper, having to be real careful not to rub my fingers across the ink else it would smudge. It read: *Two marmalade cats to give away, one boy one girl.* There was a small black and white picture of the cats, and the female's belly looked swollen.

"She's expecting," I pointed out, for no good reason 'cause Mark had already made a plan.

"Once she has her babies I'll drop them across the field for the Hewitt boys. They're a bit timid like you always were so I thought I'd help them along."

I had a vision of me and Mark in the field hanging litter after litter of kittens back when we were teenagers, and suddenly I didn't want to have that memory anymore. How come we hadn't just drowned the litters or better yet shot the momma cats that kept on having them? I was sure if we'd just shot the momma cats we could have cleaned the community in a matter of days.

Mark scratched his chin and admired the ad after I tossed it back to him, and then he decided he'd even allow Jenny to keep a kitten or two as long as there was money to have them stopped from getting pregnant.

"What about the males?" I challenged.

"Won't be us dealing with the babies."

Before I left for Eshewall that week, after Jenny had gone to school and Mark was out welding things in place, I thought about leaving a note for Jenny to reassure her I'd be back, maybe even tell her my plans to take her with me next time to the place that would be our new home. But I knew Mark would find the note no matter where I hid it, and so my words would have just been wasted.

"You sure he's feeding you proper?"

"Yes, Scott. He's feeding me like he's hoping for twins."

"I'm coming home next week to make sure, hear?"

"Yes, Scott."

"Okay, Baby. See you soon."

"Sure."

I held the receiver against my face after little Jenny hung up, listening to the static and closing my eyes to see if I couldn't trace it all the way back to the trailer kitchen where I knew she was sitting. It had been six months since I'd left for Eshewall City—Mark had been right after all, and the contract had turned into another and then another, and I hadn't been back home yet. The workdays were long there, sometimes longer than they'd been in Neverlee, but the money was getting better and better, and soon I'd have enough to put a downpayment on the nice bungalow me and Sarah had spotted on our way home from mass one Sunday. In the in-between time, I was sending money to the trailer to make sure Jenny wasn't missing anything. It was a sure way to keep her under my care in case Mark ever wanted to fight me for it. Since I wasn't showing signs of coming back too soon, though, he had backed off with his threat to take me to court over our Jenny.

I knew that was partly 'cause between me and him I was making better money, but it was mostly 'cause I was Jenny's full brother so I had rights to her. I also knew Mark had taken to stopping at the tavern every day after work. Some of the guys I had worked with in Neverlee were keeping me updated and told me Mark hadn't been promoted yet and that was making him bitter. Once or twice he phoned me in Eshewall to tell me this court person or that had come to the trailer to ask about me and made like he was getting ready to tell them the next time I had up and abandoned Jenny, but I knew he would never do that 'cause then he'd lose her too. Course they'd have every right to take little Jenny away if they found out she was expecting from a man of almost twenty-two, so I was just as guilty of keeping secrets. Thing was I had good reason, moral reason for having stayed in Eshewall longer than I had meant to. I just needed a little more time, then I could bring Jenny to a good life, marmalade cats, baby and all, and give her opportunities she had never even known to dream of.

As I sat there in the office that late winter morning, the feeling of hope infected me and suddenly I had to go back to Neverlee right then and get Jenny.

Sarah sensed my change of plans and leaned over the desk to pat my hand. "Go. Every bone in your body is grinding against the other."

Me and Sarah had met at the main office right after I came to Esh-ewall. She was the secretary, and the first time I set eyes on her I knew she was the reason I had been sent there. I mean there I was, a young man who had never had a girlfriend before, let alone allowed myself to think of having a wife someday, and there was Sarah sitting at that front desk with flowers for eyes and ribbons for hair. I knew Jenny would like her, and Sarah was excited to meet Jenny and perfectly willing to have her and her coming baby live with us.

"I could go with you," Sarah offered, even though the boss didn't like to give her time off. With a silky voice like hers answering the phones, he joked, it would be a loss to him if she were gone too long.

"No, sweetheart," I said, thinking of Sarah's best interests. "I'll be back with Jenny in a blush and then we can get all settled into our new home."

And what a perfect home it was. There was a nice green patch of front yard where Jenny would be able to sit with her baby, and plenty of space in the back for her cats to scuttle around—though I would need to talk to her about just how many cats she could have. Mark, I had heard, had let her go a bit wild with her marmalades, and I didn't want our place stinking up with litter after litter, especially since Sarah was expecting too.

So I left Eshewall by car that day, my own car and the first any man in the family had owned since I could remember, and drove with the windows down and the radio twanging the whole way to Neverlee County.

I got to say it was a bit strange passing by the projects and seeing Mark driving a bulldozer into one of the units where the roof had collapsed. There were some other guys there, too, but they were eating hot dogs and slapping each other's thighs, while Mark's torso glistened like raw steak as he gutted the proof of my first real job in Neverlee. I considered honking the horn, maybe even pulling over and getting out for a word, but I didn't have much to say to him really. The jealousy I had once felt towards him had been replaced with the more adult feeling of pity, and I didn't see any good in him being able to read that on my face.

I suppose it's no surprise when I say I felt even weirder pulling through the entrance of the trailer park. I had never driven a car through the park before, so it was something of a delicate task going between the rows of trailers. The neighbors sitting on their front steps along the way gazed with lazy interest but then looked away when I smiled, and I couldn't remember them having ever been like that with me. It had always been *Scott, good boy* or *Scott, good son* so it concerned me some when even the old lady with the Boy Scout knots for knuckles pulled the tip of her floppy hat over her face when I waved at her. Finally I thought maybe it was the car making too much noise (though the dealer had promised me it was top of the line and purred like a kitten), so I parked it in an empty lot, the Mandys' old lot, and walked the rest of the way to our trailer.

First thing I noticed was the awnings on the windows. They were full of holes like a pack of moths had been starved then set free on them. And the front step of the trailer, all around the front of the trailer for that matter, was covered in what looked like cat fur and shit. It smelled so bad I had to squirt the air around me with the breath freshener Sarah had put in my travel pack.

"Jenny?" I called, pressing my face to the screen door. The radio crackled from the kitchen and I heard water running in the bathroom, and then a few seconds later came little Jenny's pitter-patter footsteps.

"Who's there?" she asked from behind the safety of the hallway wall. I smiled at how much wiser she got every day, how clearly wise enough she had become to ask who was at the door before showing her sweet little face.

"It's me," I laughed, remembering to take my shoes off before I stepped into the trailer.

Inside, the stench of cat shit was worse, but I forced myself to breathe through my mouth so as not to make Jenny feel insulted I mightn't think she was doing a good job keeping house.

"Scott?" Jenny poked her head around the wall, and her face lit up. "Scott!" She ran over and wrapped her pipe cleaner thin arms around me.

Now me and her had never been too affectionate with each other, mostly 'cause I figured with the way the old man had been with her the last thing she wanted was me touching her too no matter which way, so I kept my arms straight until she finished her hug. Besides, except for the hard little belly sticking out from under her T-shirt there was even less of Jenny to hold onto than when I had left six months earlier.

"You sure Mark's feeding you proper?"

"Yes!" Jenny answered, a bit annoyed sounding. "There's more food in the fridge than we used to have. Go see for yourself."

"I believe you, Baby, but you're awfully skinny. Sarah'll love cooking for you."

"Sarah?"

"Sarah's my wife, but I was gonna keep that a surprise for when we got to Eshewall."

I saw the confusion start to turn Jenny's face a different color, but I can't quite describe what that color was. "Eshewall?"

"Sure, Baby. You, me and Sarah. She's real excited to meet you, and we're all gonna live together in this nice bungalow I've been saving to buy."

"What's a bunglow?"

"Bun-ga-low. You'll love it, Baby. A house all on its own with a nice big backyard just for us."

Jenny spun on a dime and went into the bathroom. I followed her up to the doorframe and extended my arms on both sides. She had filled the tub with soapy water.

"It's for the momma marmalade," she explained.

I watched Jenny lower down to her knees and make a clucking sound. Soon after, a round orange cat ran mewling between my legs and rubbed up against her belly.

"We're both expecting together," Jenny said practically, lifting the momma marmalade to her chest and placing her gently into the bathtub. I stood there all silent while she squeezed a sponge over the cat's back and then another mewl, more scratchy this one, sounded from the hallway.

"No, Buster," Jenny warned, flicking water at the male marmalade to keep him away. "This here's Lily's turn for a bath."

It took Jenny ten minutes or so to give Lily her bath, dry her off and tie a pink collar around her neck, and then she started looking for Buster, who had gotten bored and gone somewhere outside. Jenny eased down onto her hands and knees at the front of the trailer to see if Buster was underneath, and I asked her when she wanted to leave.

"Leave?"

It was as though we hadn't had a trace of that conversation back in the bathroom. "Yes, Jenny, for Eshewall. I can't be away from work too long 'cause the boss needs me to keep the crew in check."

"Then you'd better start heading back. Maybe next time you can visit longer. Heeeere, Buster! I'm sorry I got all mad at you before, but Lily was in real need of a bath."

A glance at my watch told me if Mark wasn't heading for the tavern after work then he'd be home soon, and the longer we waited the less time Jenny would have to pack what she wanted to take with her.

"Jenny! Get dressed proper and let's go." I felt a bit bad about sharpening my voice, but we had to get moving.

"I am dressed proper," was her muffled reply.

Then suddenly I lost my patience with her, the first and only time I ever did, and reached forward and yanked her to her feet, the way I had seen the old man do to Ma too many times to remember. Jenny's eyes turned white with shock, and I stumbled back a few steps 'cause it felt like Mark might have been driving his bulldozer so hard against the projects it was making the earth growl.

"Baby," I began, my voice catching 'cause I was scared she was going to start crying the way Mark used to make her. "You know I didn't mean anything by that."

But Jenny didn't start to cry. She didn't blink, and her eyes didn't even get a shine to them. Instead she took a deep breath and flattened her T-shirt over her belly and looked me square in the face. There was nothing but a slight tremor in her voice, as slight as a night's breeze during a drought.

"You left me here 'cause you was too busy making plans for some day, *some day*. Just 'cause you're ready now and you come back in a car and your shoes are all glossy don't mean you can make me leave. Mark works real hard all day doing the same thing you used to do, and he looks out for me now. He's just a little mad at life like everybody around here, but at least he came back to face it."

"It's not like that, Baby. I promise you it's not like that."

"You mightn't remember, Scott, 'cause I know you wanted so bad to erase all them memories and pretend like nothing ever happened, but I remember. I watched you help Mark hang those kittens by their throats out there in the field so don't you go pretending you're all proper. You ain't my Pa."

Jenny shook her head as if to get rid of the memory, then Buster came running over to her and she picked up her marmalade cat, the marmalade cat I never got for her, and brought him back into the trailer.

RUNAWAYBITCH13

runawaybitch13 (9:06 pm):
u there?

Dargelos23 (9:06 pm):
yeah

runawaybitch13 (9:06 pm):
sorry we had a fight 2day

Dargelos23 (9:06 pm):
we did?

runawaybitch13 (9:07 pm):
didnt we?

Dargelos23 (9:07 pm):
i guess. im sorry 2

In grade seven, the worst grade of my life until I met Justin, there were three other M—'s in my class. M— Grant who stuffed her bra for science class with Mr. Andrews, M— Frank who went to third base with her brother on Friday nights after their father went drinking for boys' night, and M— Smith who I felt bad for because there was nothing remarkable about her and everybody wants to leave their mark in the world. My homeroom teacher laughed like I had told some sort of cute joke when I decided to change my name, and then she had the balls to tell the class how when she was thirteen she had fantasized about changing her name too because she thought it would improve her. She didn't believe me when I said my self-esteem wasn't the issue. The first time I signed a test with my new name, Miss Folio put an X over it and gave me zero on ten even though I had spelled every word perfect including the bonus word *deceet*.

Then she called my parents in for a parent-teacher meeting, and I had to sit outside the classroom while she yapped away, and then my parents came out all sour-faced and took me home in the kind of silence that usually meant *you're grounded*. When we got home, my father asked if everybody wanted pizza, which was ridiculous because "everybody" was just us because my grandmother had D—, and so I knew Miss Fucking Folio had told some lie about me. While we waited for the pizza to arrive, my parents decided we should all sit in the living room and have a family moment.

"Are dark colors the new trend?" my mother asked.

"No."

"Is that what the cool kids wear now?" my father asked.

"They're not cool."

"What happened to the pink scarf your grandmother knitted?" my mother asked.

"I don't know."

"Why?" my father asked.

"Because."

When the pizza arrived, my father tipped the deliveryman with pocket change like he was giving him diamonds, and my mother set the dinner table as if this was a hugely important task. She fluttered around the kitchen collecting plates, utensils, cups, and flat soda, all jumpy and round-bellied like a robin in her countryside apron. Whenever we went shopping I tried to make her get something new, like a V-neck instead of a turtleneck or a pair of jeans instead of corduroys with patches sewn on the knees to make them look used, but her excuse was always the same: She preferred life's little simplicities and these fads I went through, these "stages of life", would eventually become tiresome to me and I would find pleasure in the same things as her. Holy fuck, my grandmother had better sense.

Anyway, the pizza arrived and we ate it, and then came more questions.

"You wear makeup now," my mother said.

"It's eyeliner."

"Why? Your face is so pretty all natural," my father said.

"Like my *name*?"

I felt bad slapping him like that. Of course I didn't really slap him, but that's how it looked because he squinted and patted his cheek. But then that was complete BS because my father could make himself cry on command. He would do it for fun sometimes, like when we played a game of Risk and I won, though most times he did it when he wanted something from my mother, like sex or forgiveness for not coming straight home after boys' night with M— Frank's father. I don't know, to tell you the truth, if my father had any real sad feelings about anything except for the night he got lost on a winter hunting trip with his friend Jeffrey. I think he really regretted it when the rescue team found Jeffrey with only some bottom teeth left where his head used to be—he'd chomped down good on his .45-70 lever-action rifle because he'd been too scared of a little frostbite. Plus they had been hunting protected bison so my father got a double fine for him and his dead accomplice.

"What's wrong with your name, M—?"

"It's common."

My mother took me shopping the next day after school, pretending she wanted to have a girls' afternoon. That's where I met Justin, at the department store that day, while my mother tried on a pair of stone-washed straight out of an eighties ad with Patrick Swayze.

"Can I help you with anything, *madame*?"

Who the fuck calls a teenage girl *madame* except a French person from another century, a high-school loser, or somebody different, maybe even a little exciting? Justin, as his department store nametag said, wasn't French as far as I could tell because he didn't have one of those thin greasy moustaches and didn't smell like bad cheese, he was too old to be a high-school loser plus his eyebrow and nose were pierced and I was sure he was wearing mascara because no guy could possibly have long black eyelashes like Justin did, especially a guy with bleach blond hair, so basically he had to be somebody different.

"I'd like to get out of this stupid store and out of this buttfuck boring town. Could you help me with that?"

I know I impressed Justin. It was so obvious from the way he stared at me like I had just appeared out of nowhere. He knew right away that I was smart for my age, smarter than Miss Fucking Folio and everybody else at my school, smarter than my parents. According to science I was smarter than my Downs brother, D—, but science isn't always right. So D— had a total vocabulary of five words and looked like a little old man even though he was eight. He was also super-sharp and super-sensitive to everything that went on around him, and that was why he stayed with my grandmother most of the time. The shit that went on in my house made D— have seizures, and he needed to be protected from that— from our asinine parents whose faults it was that he had Downs in the first place. If my mother hadn't popped all those pills that she claimed saved her from the "horrors of pregnancy" the whole time D— was in her, he would have been born perfectly normal like me.

I didn't think Justin was cute at first. It was the way he showed appreciation for what I said, hung onto all of my words, spoke to me like I was mature and agreed that black was so my color. And he was reasonable about my mother even though I wanted him to find her as lame as I did.

"Let her buy some jeans for herself. It's important for ladies to buy clothes, especially when their daughters are so pretty and they feel like they need to keep up. It's only natural, ya know?"

Justin was a good salesman. He had my mother singing like a hopped-up canary at the cash register, had her opening her wallet and smiling and blushing even though he wore earrings and mascara and a chain around his waist instead of a belt.

"What a pleasant young man," she said on the drive home.

"Can we go back tomorrow?"

"It's quite a drive."

"But the T-shirt I want will be there because Justin ordered it specially for me."

"Justin?"

As usual in winter when there was no fresh snow to plough, my father was asleep in front of the TV when we got home. My mother made a shush motion with her hand and flicked my cheek when I kicked my boots off against the wall. "*Don't* wake your father up."

She glared at me like my very existence was offensive. My mother could turn vicious just like that, especially when my father was out of work. In a way it made sense because he could turn pretty vicious himself without much warning, especially if he was disturbed from an afternoon snooze, which was usually grounds for lots of yelling and things flying through the air. Because D— was so small and attracted to loud noises and moving objects, my grandmother always worried that my father would hurl him through the air, mistaking him for one of my mother's fake potted cacti or ceramic farm animals arranged in these tacky Bible scenes all over the house. Not because he would mean to, he was actually very protective of D— and would crack anybody in the jaw for making fun of him, but when my father was unemployed he seemed to need other ways to exercise his authority over us and he was a very different person in those instances. I remember my mother crouching in a corner of the room once with her hands over her head while my father raged about losing his job again, like she thought if she could make herself small like D— then my father wouldn't use her as a demonstration of his power. I don't think she ever crouched in a corner again after that.

I suddenly missed D— even though he had spent the weekend over, missed his little old-man feet knocking into each other as he waddle-galloped over to me with his arms flopping up and down like baby chicken wings before they grow feathers. He had this hideous laugh like a congested donkey that I loved so much because it was laughter that never pretended to be something it wasn't. Also, when D— was at our house there was a sort of truce in the air because the moments were numbered and things become valuable once they're numbered. My grandmother basically had full custody of him, but she would leave him with us for a week straight when my parents were in good shape. Her standards were more lenient than the social worker's. My grandmother eventually convinced the child welfare people to ease up until finally the social worker stopped making surprise visits and kept to a schedule that we could all prepare for.

"Go to your room," my mother said. All I did was open my mouth, and she clipped my ear between her thumb and forefinger and twisted so hard that I folded sideways.

"Ouch!"

Well that did it. My father's eyes popped open, and my mother slapped me across the face. "How dare you talk to me like that!"

She could be amazingly dumb, my mother. Included in her ways of avoiding a confrontation with my father was inventing some situation where I had caused trouble and then looking to my father for help disciplining me. Sometimes he would, if he was ready to lay down the law at that particular moment, but he always got her later anyways.

"What is it this time?"

"I took her all the way to the department store and now she wants to go back tomorrow because some guy, a *cashier*, says he'll have something for her. I bet he has something for her."

My father was in one of his *laissez-faire* moods that day. In fact I think he might have been clinically depressed because the town hadn't called him for work all week. "I'll take her then if it's too much trouble after you've been sitting on your ass all day polishing the shine right out of the coffee table while you watch that Christ shit."

I walked down the hallway to my bedroom, and my mother mouthed *sorry* to me when my father wasn't watching. In return, I fanned my hands in the air and gave her the finger. Twice.

I stayed in my room and listened to music all night and trimmed my hair to make it more interesting because it was just long and brown, and I thought I should have a new look for Justin. Then I put together the perfect outfit: black jeans with a hole in one knee and the crotch, red stockings for underneath so I wouldn't look trashy sitting with my legs open, and a black turtleneck. I might sound like a hypocrite because I was always trying to make my mother wear V-necks instead of turtlenecks, but there was no point in me flashing around my totally flat chest. Maybe it would always stay flat and eventually become a sagging blob of deflated skin like my mother's, but I really didn't care. I knew that the boys who liked girls for their low-cut tops and tissue-filled bras were creeps, and I was not interested in creeps. This girl in my grade seven class who sometimes talked to me at recess wore frilly see-thru tops all the time. I liked her even though she was a total drooling idiot for boys. She always had a good book with her, and Miss Folio was always scolding her in homeroom for reading the book instead of listening to the daily announcements. This one book had a character I knew I would fall in love with if I met him in real life: Dargelos, this loner-type in a black trench coat who went around eliminating people that the world could do without. Frilly Girl left the book on her desk one recess, and after I read the first few chapters I decided that I would find a boyfriend exactly like Dargelos.

My father was gone to work the next morning because it had snowed, and I could just imagine his joy when he woke up and saw a million white particles outside his window blowing around so thick that the world looked like a piece of Styrofoam. My mother always got anxious when my father went out in the plough, and her solution was always to stay busy, so there was a fresh warm breakfast of griddlecakes and scrambled eggs waiting for me in the kitchen.

"Juice, M—?"

"I am not M—."

"Fine, Not-M—. Juice?"

"No."

"I wish the town would buy a new plough. Your father will end up in a ditch."

"I'm sure you'd get widow's comp."

"M—!"

"I am not M—." I helped myself to griddlecakes and the rest of the maple syrup.

"Fuck, M—, I just don't know what to do with you."

"What's there to do?"

"We're trying, we really are, but you insist on being such a little bitch and I'm afraid the child welfare people will take you away like they did your brother."

It had never crossed my mind that I could also go live with my grandmother. You'd think it would have, since apparently that was an option, but I had figured the reason D— was taken away was because he was handicapped and my parents couldn't deal with that. I hadn't realized that maybe they just couldn't deal with being parents at all. I ate my griddlecakes and thought about living with my grandmother and decided that I liked my house better. But what if my grandmother and D— moved in and my parents left? It's amazing how once an idea pops into your head it can just grow and expand until it's all you can think about. Finally I promised my mother I would be nicer, but she had to promise me something.

"What?" She dabbed her eyes in Hollywood fashion like she thought all it took was waterworks and an apology to re-establish order in our house.

"I want to go to the department store by myself after school."

"Why?"

"Because."

"I don't know."

"Please?" Sometimes I look back and think, if I had used that word more often then things could have turned out very differently.

"Home by suppertime or else. Got it?"

Naturally I was going straight to the department store. I didn't know if Justin would be there in the morning, but I was prepared to sit in the diner across the street and wait all day if I had to, and drink coffee and read that girl's book about Dargelos that I still had from that recess she left it on her desk.

Miskwi, the town where I grew up, has a population of two thousand and is cut off from the rest of the world by the Miskwi River. There are no mountains, no valleys, no forests, just boring agriculture like maize, squash, and beans. Every few miles there are wooded patches that look like pubic hair if you happen to be in a helicopter, and protected bison roam between the wooded areas like crabs from one gnarly patch to another. How the fuck people ended up north of the Miskwi River never made its way into history, not even the town's, and so everybody is just there, rootless even though they've never been anywhere else. Nobody new ever comes to Miskwi except government workers who get posted for six months at a time to observe because, of course, only freaks live in a town like Miskwi. The two most popular ways to leave are join the army or commit a crime to end up at the Miskwi House of Corrections and hope that when you're paroled you get integrated into a community south of the river where the world begins. Everybody wants to leave Miskwi, but nobody has the money to pick up and start a new life somewhere else, and it's impossible to get south of the river without a helicopter.

A tenth of the people are natives and keep to themselves in these long fishy rowhouses that you can smell from miles away and are filled with families of twenty or more—great-grandparents, grandparents, mothers and fathers, and screeching children who run outside in the middle of winter in T-shirts and barefoot. The rowhousers have their own school and their own police. They hunt, fish and pick their food, and they hold some kind of ritualistic bonfire every week that everybody else in the town can see clawing at the midnight sky. My mother hated the rowhousers—"featherbrains" she called them. She said she wasn't a racist and would accept their way of life with open arms if they would accept hers and attend church every Sunday with the rest of the townspeople to prove they had the same values and morals as we did. No true racist would ever be willing to share their House of God. My father didn't go to church, and I stopped as soon as I was old enough to understand what a waste of time it is watching some dusty old priest whine about how important it is to confess your sins if you want to be pardoned on Judgment Day, and then appoint himself the vessel of God that could help save you. I hoped Armageddon would happen right in my living room like a pay-per-view, and a giant hand would squash my parents and lift me out of that shithole and reunite me with D—, and from there we'd go out into the world and see what there was for us.

The townspeople of Miskwi are totally lame and their kids are all stupid, at least the ones who don't hang themselves with their bed sheets the way some inmates at the House of Corrections do when they realize that life north of the river, inside or out, is worse than death. If you're a man you'll most likely be seasonally employed by the town like my father was, plough snow and break ice in the winter and grow produce the rest of the year that isn't worth exporting so everybody ends up eating the same three things all fucking year round—squash stew, bean casserole, and cornbread. You'll also go to Spitz, the only place that serves hard liquor, which is brought to your table by delinquent rowhouse girls who might as well be wearing napkins because they know the townsmen secretly like their red skin and will tip a little extra if they can touch it. Sometimes the rowhouse girls came to my school as part of a cultural exchange program, and I think the program was a hoax because we never got to learn anything about their culture and most of what they learned about ours was how mean townies are. Once there was this girl named Mitena who let me try some of her homemade hominy bread. She was only at school that one day, a Friday, and the next Monday all the kids in my class were flapping around the room because somebody's father had left a newspaper clipping out about a girl who had been branded and dipped in gasoline after she left Spitz Saturday night, and the picture—of her before she caught fire—looked exactly like Mitena. I don't know if it was her, but she never came back and usually rowhousers stayed at my school for a week.

This might seem way off topic, but it's important that you get a visual of my buttfuck boring town so you can understand how excited I was to go to the department store to see Justin. The second I stepped out of my house I felt freed, like I had cut all ties with everything that went on inside and I was on my way to a new life, a life of surprises and crazy adventures with a guy who had fallen in love with me the day before, almost like we were these wild animals that had found each other in a land full of raccoons and other scavengers who didn't need to be part of each other like we did in order to survive.

Miskwi High is a few miles outside the town on a road that leads to the department store if you follow it to the end, and Checkerz Diner is right across. Now that I think of it, nobody put any effort into urban planning or whatever it's called when you design a town for convenience because there is no logical reason why three of the town's most used buildings are so out of the way. Supposedly the department store is out of the way so kids can't play hooky during school or hang out there on weekends and make the place dirtier than it is, but they do anyways and nobody who works at the department store is about to report that, because they're grateful to have jobs and know their place.

It occurred to me after I got off the school bus and hid behind a snow bank until all the kids were in class that Justin might be new in town. That made him even more exciting, the fact that I got him first. I had never heard any of the girls in my class talk about the bleach blond guy at the department store, and those girls talked about everything. I could just imagine their fat little red cheeks getting fatter and redder when they showed up at the store later and saw me and Justin walking towards the diner for his break, holding hands and laughing like we had known each other forever. The girls in my school always got involved with boys in the school, usually in the same class, and you can only guess the kinds of idiotic problems that caused. Homeroom could be a warzone if a couple had just broken up and Miss Folio, the only time I ever cheered for her, had to referee nasty fights that often got physical. I have to hand it to her that she was not afraid to get down and dirty in those instances and squeeze herself between feuding lovers and pry them apart with her skinny arms like she was the Jaws of Life.

Justin pretended not to notice when I got to the department store, but it was so obvious that he saw me. One second he was pulling the tips of his hair into teeth like a crosscut saw at the top of his head and the next he was counting the money in his cash register even though not a single item had been sold because the store had just opened. I understood his need for a distraction though and decided I needed a reason other than him to be at the store, so I began winding my way up and down the aisles of the men's section like I had a purpose. The section was exactly two and a half aisles including accessories like belts and wallets that all looked the same even though they were different prices. The rest was all for women including the obnoxious perfume·section where a girl I recognized from elementary school stood behind the counter spritzing herself and reeking up the whole department store. When Justin moved his attention from his cash register to something else, I continued on to visit the perfume counter.

"You're M— Richards from grade six, right?" the girl working there said.

"Uh, H—?"

"Yessss! Ohmygod*hi!*"

"Uh, hi. What's, uh, what's new?" I stared at H—'s stomach. She was able to hide it as long as she pressed herself against the service counter, which was waist-high, but as soon as she moved her arms or backed up just an inch, the hard, low-set melon of her belly was so obvious that I almost felt awkward in her place.

H— looked down. "I work with my mom. We need the extra money, you know, for the family, since my dad's lumber accident."

I had totally forgot about H—'s father, which had been a huge ordeal just a few months earlier. Nobody in town had seen him in person since he returned home from his lumber job so people had started the rumor that he had died on the job and left his family hard up. A few lucky men leave Miskwi for six months each year to work in oil or lumber and make enough money to provide for their families for the rest of the year. They don't have to lift a finger when they're back in town, just sleep in, drink, fish and hunt with their buddies and occasionally try to create more children. H—'s father had been known as a decent man, not interested in slacking off when he was home with his family and never laying eyes or hands on anybody but his wife and kids and only in the most decent of ways. In elementary school, H— always had the most appetizing lunches, and every Friday her mother packed a bag of candies for her to share with the class at recess. Even without her candies H— was very nice, and nobody can fault a person who's nice. She was pretty too, with the long wheat-colored hair and iceberg-blue eyes that every girl wishes for in secret. The mean girls were stumped coming up with insults for H—, and what they thought were their best ones—Ice Queen and Prairie Dog—only served to bring her more to the attention of boys who liked those features in a girl. I didn't talk to H— much, except when she offered me candies or asked about D—, who she was interested in because her plan was to become a counselor for special needs people. It really was too bad to see her now working in the perfume section of the department store, and I was quite sure this was because her mother had pulled her out of school faster than an oil fire spreads and forced her to work in a location where she would be on display to all of her old friends like a highway billboard for bad teenage behavior.

H— rattled away about some news story she had heard about the rowhouse people getting a chunk of money from the government, but I couldn't help myself from looking over at Justin.

"You know him?" she asked.

"He said he'd have this T-shirt today that I want."

"Justin's nice, but his mom is *wacked*. She comes to get him after work and sits in her car and honks the horn until he closes up his cash and stuff."

"I just want my shirt. Nice seeing you, H—. I hope you do all right."

"I like working here. Do you want something? Anything? I get free samples." H— opened one of the counter drawers and grabbed a handful of makeup and perfume samples. She spread them across the counter so fast a couple skidded right off, and then she swept her arms wide and invited me to take whatever I wanted.

"I don't wear makeup."

"Yes you do. Here. A specialty eyeliner that women pay big money for. You can have it. For free!"

"No thanks."

"Please, *please* have some." H—'s eyes were filling with tears with so much determination that I took pity on her. I knew it was the hormones making her like that because my father had told me how wild my mother was when she was pregnant with me, and I sort of remembered her many states when she was carrying D—. I took the eyeliner H— waved at me and when she turned to greet a shopper on the other side of the counter, I lifted a mascara because I figured Justin deserved it for putting up with a bitch for a mother.

What can I say about the first time we actually talked to each other? Nothing to do with the store or my T-shirt, nothing to do with anything but ourselves and how bad we had fallen for each other the day before and how that one night in between had been the longest night of the year. I had to wait until Justin's lunch break for this to take place so I went across the street to Checkerz and sipped black coffee that tasted like feet. Have you ever been in love? I mean the kind of love that exists outside your head and silly fantasies, the kind that *materializes* and makes you a better person when you're around the person you're in love with? There is no in-between or less-than if you're in love, and the best way to tell if you are is to identify that feeling of danger that first popped into your head like every other idea does before it becomes a feeling if it's meant to. So many people say they're in love when really they're lying just to make themselves important. The people who lie about it have never been in love and never will be—they're so obsessed with appearing happy that they send happiness itself flying right over their heads like those cheap boomerangs that never come back to you after you fling them and so you realize you've wasted a month's allowance.

That Justin might not come to Checkerz for his lunch break only occurred to me after I was at the diner with my order placed. I had lifted ten bucks from my mother's wallet before I left that morning, but I didn't exactly want to spend it all at the diner for nothing. Checkerz was, in the world of diners, the most basic kind: six tables for two along a wall of windows that offered a crappy view of the department store, which was as crappy as the diner and everything else in the town. The tables were the folding kind set up for old people who play cards or hold bazaars in church basements, the kind with legs that never stand perfectly straight and collapse all the time for no reason. The chairs were also folding and you could end up on your ass if you coughed or sat too close to the edge. On the opposite wall was a long metal-top counter with a cash register at one end and a pyramid of "Out of Order" candy dispensers at the other. There was a pastel anthill on the bottom of one of the dispensers, like maybe once it had been a mountain of sour suckers that had been faded and baked right to dust year after year from the sun. The cook and waitress both worked behind the counter, and the way they moved and chatted like they were in some corny movie where the diner was the main attraction made me want to hurl. There was not one fucking interesting thing about Checkerz, not a fake plant, fake artwork, fake jukebox, not even a newspaper clipping about how amazing the diner was, written by a restaurant critic who was secretly best friends with the owner. Checkerz was not a proud establishment, and this was reflected in the dull employees and the two losers sitting at the counter in fur hats with earflaps talking about the newest Spitz girl.

I was never more bored in my life than that morning in Checkerz. I even got bored of reading about Dargelos and closed the book when I would have ordinarily been totally sucked in. It's not that I didn't enjoy the idea of poison and blackmail, but the reality was that I was being made to wait for a hugely anticipated moment and I was growing pissed. The thought did cross my mind that Justin was making me wait on purpose. I mean, don't people who work full days get more than a lunch break? Nobody in their right mind can be expected to work in a depressing place like the department store and be nice to bullshit customer after bullshit customer without breaks. I knew I would never be able to work at the department store or anywhere that required me to be polite to people all for the sake of getting their money.

To give you an exact picture of how things were when finally Justin walked in is only to your benefit. These kinds of details are the most memorable kind, the ones you want to tell and retell for the rest of your life when they happen to you. Until they do, you're best learning from another person's experience. Justin walked in so quiet that the bells above the diner door barely jingled, and he looked official and mysterious with his black bomber jacket unzipped just enough to show his store nametag. The cook waved at him, and the waitress poured him a coffee immediately. Justin sat on a counter stool, closed his hands around the coffee mug, and became small and round like a turtle as if all of his morning tensions caught up to him at once. Knowing what I did about him already, that his mother was crazy, I didn't want to interrupt him too soon. A person needs time to detox from misery, and it was essential that Justin knew I was aware of this, and the only way to let him know was to do right by not bothering him. He had seen me when he came into the diner, so it was a matter of patience on my part.

"Aren't you supposed to be in school, *mademoiselle*?" When finally he joined me, Justin was smiling like everything we said or did from that moment on would be an inside joke that nobody would ever be able to rip off.

"I liked it better when you called me *madame*."

"Sorry, *madame*. And does *madame* have a name?"

"Yes."

"And would she like to tell me before I go back to work?"

"M—."

"And would *Madame* M— like to meet me after work?"

"Why?"

"To tell me more about why she's so damn sexy." The more we talked, the quieter and shyer Justin got, as if his whispery way wasn't quiet enough already. By the time he went to leave we were practically speaking in sign language—touching, holding hands, locking fingers. When Justin leaned over to kiss the top of my head, a perfectly normal way to kiss a girl on a first date, his store nametag dangled in my face and behind it was a perfume-sample sized vial filled with red liquid. I have to admit that I felt jealous because maybe H— had given it to him, which meant maybe they had a relationship which H— had not said a word about when we had talked about Justin just that morning, so I was silently preparing to have a word with her if this turned out to be true.

I tugged on the vial. "What's this?"

Justin pulled back and zipped his bomber jacket so fast his shirt got jammed.

"Justin?"

"I'll tell you later, where it's more private."

"But I want to know now."

"Not here."

"I won't come see you if you don't tell me."

Justin sat down again. He seemed nervous, maybe even irritated with me, but I had a right to know since he had just kissed me.

"It's blood."

"What is?"

"In the vial, it's blood. I have a vial of blood around my neck be-cause I'm a three-hundred-year-old werewolf."

"There's no such thing."

"Yes there is. Ever heard of the disease called Lupus?"

"Yes."

"So there's such a thing, right?"

"Yes."

"I have Lupus, only the Western world doesn't believe in werewolves so it had to find another term for the disease, ya know, for the people who can't handle what it really is."

"So do you, like, turn into a wolf?"

"When I have a Lupus attack, but I don't *look* like a wolf, exactly."

"Is the blood like your medicine?"

"All the questions!"

"I want to know, Justin!"

"Yes, it's like my medicine. Still want to come see me after work?"

I leaned across the table and pulled Justin forward until his mouth was smack on mine.

runawaybitch13 (9:07 pm):
when ur, u know, a werewolf r u dangerous?

Dargelos23 (9:07 pm):
can b. why?

runawaybitch13 (9:08 pm):
how much longer will u b 1?

Dargelos23 (9:08 pm):
dunno, not long. im starting 2 feel better

A week into our relationship, Justin felt it was time to introduce me to his mother if I was going to be meeting him at the department store every day after school. I'm happy to report that the encounter went perfectly despite what H— had said about her (in truth H— was jealous in advance of girls who might want to get with Justin so she made up lies to scare them off). Glory said I was a "loquacious young lady" (that means chatty, which goes to show how right Justin was for me because I was not a chatty person), and I would be good for her son because he was such the quiet type that when he was an infant she had worried he might be retarded.

"I knew that was because it was just the two of us, and a baby needs both a mother and father to have a normal development, but I would be damned bringing just any man into our home and exposing my son to the revolving door of relationship tragedy."

"Mother."

"Well it's true. I had already done wrong by getting involved with that rat-ass son of a bitch who isn't even your father because I told the doctor I didn't know where you came from, so I wasn't about to bring some leech into the home who thought he'd get lucky off my disability pension or family allowance. It almost doubled, you know, that pension, after you were born."

Justin and his mother lived in a featureless gray portable that neighbored with a bunch of other deserted ones. The government had evicted those families with plans to donate the portables to the rowhousers who were willing to assimilate, but Glory had remained firmly in place and was even preparing a lawsuit against the government for trying to displace a disabled single mother. I don't know the technical word for what was wrong with her, but she was in pretty bad shape and looked a lot older than I bet she was. She had a rusted oxygen tank with a slimy yellowed tube hooked to the insides of her nostrils, her wrists and ankles were in bandages, and her belly flopped over the waist of her drawstring sweatpants and hung towards the ground like there was a weight attached to it. To make up for her inability to do much physical activity, Glory read a lot, which was how she knew words like loquacious. Her favorite kind of book was the detective novel.

"Ever read one, M—?"

"No."

"Maybe detectives aren't cool for your age group."

"I don't know."

"What is your age group, M—?"

"Stop with the questions, Mother."

"I'm just asking."

"Well stop."

Justin started to roll a cigarette and Glory tapped him on the hand. He continued to roll and Glory tapped him again, but he was standing his ground. I can't say I disagreed with him even though I wanted him to quit that filthy habit, because there Glory was wheezing away as she adjusted her oxygen tube with one hand and smoked her own cigarette with the other.

"So, M—, do you go to the high school?"

"Yes."

"What grade are you in?"

"Mother!"

Justin leapt to his feet and pulled me with him. He was a strong guy considering how skinny he was. He was as pale as he was skinny, but he didn't get that from his mother. Glory had dark, heavy features, a Roman nose I think they're called, puffy chewed-up lips and stiff black hair. The only thing Justin seemed to have inherited from her was illness. When we were in his room, which was in truth a walk-in closet with a single mattress on the floor and an upside-down plastic milk crate with an ashtray and an old laptop on it, I followed up on Glory's questions.

"How old are you, Justin?"

"It doesn't matter. We get each other."

"We do?"

"Do you see me asking how old you are?"

"No."

"And do you know why?"

"Because you know?"

"No, I don't know, M—. I'm not a psychic."

"Sorry."

"Because it doesn't matter. I already told you I'm a three-hundred-year-old werewolf and that doesn't matter to you. Or does it?"

Justin had this super-intense way of staring when he was being subjected to questions he did not want to answer. His eyes bulged big and round and didn't blink, just stared at you cold like a corpse until you found yourself at a loss for words. He could win any conversation that way so you had to be absolutely sure going in that you would not wimp out or back down because you only got one chance.

"I'm thirteen, Justin."

"I said I don't care."

"I'm thirteen and I love you and I know you love me too."

"Stop it, M—. Stop it!"

"You are going to be my first, Justin. There has never been anybody else, and I want you to be my first."

Justin had been typing away on his laptop, having one of his quiet tantrums, but he stopped as soon as I brought up sex. Now understand that I was not offering sex in that moment. In fact I would not offer sex until the perfect moment and I wasn't ready to share my plan with him just yet, but I figured the best way to show him how serious I was about him was to put the promise out there.

"What's on the computer that's more important than me, Justin?"

"I'm signing you up with WolfDen."

"What's that?"

"A place where we can be together even when we can't see each other."

"Like for werewolves and their freak girlfriends?"

"Yeah. So you see, sexy, nothing's more important than you."

Just like I wasn't the "loquacious" type, I wasn't the squealing type, but there I was suddenly making these embarrassing girl sounds and smothering Justin onto his mattress and kissing his face like I had a kissing problem. "We're too good for this buttfuck town and our shit families."

Justin rolled on top of me and kissed me back. "Maybe we should leave." He tasted like bad Indian cigarettes and his hair smelled like H—'s department store perfume of the day, but I loved him anyway. He was the most exciting person I had ever known and I would do anything for him.

When I got home that night my parents were arguing about which movie they were going to watch with D—. My mother thought an action movie would induce one of his seizures since he reacted badly to loud crashing things, and my father thought a cartoon would make him have a seizure because a newspaper article he had read recently claimed that bright colors agitated young children. My mother said over her dead body would they watch a romance because the last thing she needed was a child with Downs getting ideas about intimacy, and my father refused to watch a comedy. Period. I wanted to hurl, watching them argue and thump around the living room like overgrown children who didn't have the vocabulary to properly express themselves. Couldn't they see? Couldn't they fucking well see that no matter what movie they watched D— would have a fucking seizure? If they seriously didn't know by then that D—'s seizures were his way of saying, "Get me the fuck out of this house," then my parents didn't deserve to have him for one more minute. The whole time, my little brother was lying on his stomach on the floor, flailing his arms and legs around, gasping and gurgling up his supper and unable to get himself upright because he needed help but my parents were too busy yelling. I fucking hated them. I wanted them to die. I scooped D— up myself and brought him to my room. After I cleaned him up, he rolled around on my bed and laughed while I chatted online with Justin, and I started to think how nice it would be if we took D— with us when we left.

"I'd have to drink his blood," Justin said the next day at lunch.

"Just because I don't know a whole lot about werewolves doesn't mean I don't know the difference."

"What difference?"

"Between werewolves and vampires. If you were a vampire you'd have to drink his blood."

"There's no such thing as vampires."

"Is too. There's a TV show all about them and it has a werewolf."

"M—, seriously."

"What?"

"You need to learn the difference between fiction and reality."

We had a stormy relationship, Justin and I, but relationships where nobody ever speaks their mind or argues always end in utter disaster. There are top stories in the news all the time about some man, a perfectly ordinary man with no history of violence, who suddenly snaps one day and does something impulsive and extreme like blows up his wife or chops her into bits along with all of the children and makes a stew with them. Sometimes you hear about women doing horrible things too, except that women seem to be better able to suck it in and wait for the perfect moment to increase their chances of not getting found out. Fighting can also be a sign of trouble in the relationship, like my parents, the Ongoing Spectacle of Total Failure, but Justin and I didn't fight like them. The signature of our arguments was that they lasted forever because neither of us was the type to back down easily. One of our biggest issues was that Justin thought nobody got him, although that was really his issue except that in a relationship all issues become shared.

"I get you Justin. And who else are you talking about? You say all the time that you hate people and you don't have any friends, so who is there to not get you?"

"The reason I have no friends is *because* nobody gets me, M—. There's a difference. And I don't hate people, I just hate the ones who don't get me. And you don't really get me either or else you wouldn't be asking me what I'm talking about."

That was the wrong thing for Justin to say to me, especially on our one-month anniversary. I had gone out of my way for the occasion, walked to the department store during school lunch to bring him left-over lasagna and garlic bread from supper the night before, and I had even made him a personalized card with a picture of Peter Stubbe, the world's first werewolf from Germany.

"You're a dick." I shoved Justin's anniversary surprise at him, but he grabbed it before I could smear his face with it.

His nose twitched. "What is this?"

"Open it and find out, dumbass."

With just the tips of his fingers, Justin peeled away the tin foil. Then he yelped and threw my gift on the floor and ducked behind his service counter. "Get it away! Get it away!"

I picked up the lunch and leaned over the counter. "What the fuck's wrong with you?"

Justin pointed at the lunch and fanned the air spastically. "Garlic! Garlic!"

"So?"

"I'm allergic! I'm allergic!"

"Oh." The closest garbage can was at the front of the store. Justin was leaning against his counter and trembling when I got back to him.

"Never *ever* bring garlic near me again, understand? Did you eat any before you kissed me? Tell me you didn't eat any. Oh God!"

"Sorry, I didn't know."

Justin threw his hand across his forehead like a black and white movie star about to faint, and I hate to admit it but for a second he looked really gay.

"You *did* eat garlic before you kissed me!"

Before I could tell him no I didn't, he ripped the vial from his neck and drank the blood, which looked sort of silly since the vial was the size of a perfume sample and so he didn't really drink from it but sucked on it like a miniature straw. Right after, he pressed his hands on his counter, closed his eyes, and counted to ten. When he opened his eyes he seemed calmer, maybe even a little high. He reached for my hand and squeezed it between both of his.

"M—," he began, in a tone like a grown-up about to explain something complicated to a child, "I should have told you so it's my fault. Of all the things in the world that could harm me, garlic is number one."

"Do you have other allergies?"

"What do you mean?"

"I read that people with Lupus have all kinds of allergies so you should tell me now so I don't accidentally kill you or something."

"I wasn't having a Lupus attack, M—."

"I don't get it."

Justin lifted my hand to his mouth and kissed it. His lips felt like peeling wood.

"*Madame* sexy M—, to truly get me you have to understand that I'm a three-hundred-year-old werewolf."

"I know that."

"Werewolves and garlic don't mix."

"But. Uh. Okay, fine."

One day not long after, Justin had a Lupus attack. H— balled her eyes out as she told me about it when I arrived at the department store after school.

"It was awful. The skin on his face, like on his nose and cheeks, suddenly turned red. So red! And it got all scaly like it would fall off if you touched it."

"Where is he now?" I was pretty sure H— didn't know that Justin was a werewolf, in fact I don't even think Glory knew what his Lupus really was, so it was absolutely necessary that I find out where he had gone to hide.

"The employee room but I don't know if he's still there because he made me promise not to let anybody in and I haven't seen him since."

"Where's the employee room?"

"You can't go in there, M—. It's for employees only." H— had turned cold with me ever since I started with Justin, and in return I had lost all pity for her situation. Whenever I went to the store, she had something snippy and disapproving to say to me, and I was at the point where I couldn't be nice to her anymore.

"Where is the employee room, *cashier girl*?"

"He's too old for you and he's not interested, he's just nice and it's too bad you can't tell the difference."

"M—, sexy, you're here!"

We turned to see Justin limping towards us, and it was a sight sad enough to end the most vicious of fights. Like H— had said, the skin on Justin's face was red and scaly and in the shape of a butterfly or something like it. In my opinion he looked less like a werewolf and more like a burn victim, but I wasn't going to bring that up in such a delicate situation. Justin's lips were super puffy, and I think maybe his tongue was swollen because he slurred when he spoke, and he swayed against a cane that still had a price tag hanging from the handgrip.

"Justin?"

Justin limped over to me and dropped his head on my shoulder. His breath rolled out in great big trembles, and his whole body felt so hot he must have had a dangerous fever. "Go outside and tell my mom to come in. Tell her to bring the blanket."

"Blanket?"

"I can't be in sunlight when I'm like this."

H— stared at us without shame and then barged in like the hungry little jackal she was as soon as I turned to leave. "Do you need anything, Justin? Do you want to sit behind the counter with me?"

Justin ignored her and blew me a kiss. It clearly took his every last effort to make the gesture because next he started to cough and speckled bloody mucus all over H—'s white blouse.

The Lupus attack lasted two weeks and in those two weeks we became closer than you could ever imagine. Glory picked me up every day after school and drove me most of the way home in time for supper, though I think the only reason she went out of her way like that was because she didn't want to take care of her sick son. I mean sure she had her own health problems to care for, but in truth she was more interested in reading her bargain bin detective novels and chain smoking. (Justin, by the way, stopped smoking cigarettes while he was sick, and I was so proud of him that I let him get to second base with me when he started feeling better.)

"I think I'll go back to work tomorrow."

"Are you sure, Justin?"

"I can't stand being cooped up anymore. I'd rather melt in the sun."

"When will you feel good enough to leave?"

"Leave?"

"Like we talked about. *Leaving.*"

"I think I'd rather stay here."

"Justin."

"You don't really want to leave, sexy. You told me you like your house and D—, it's just your parents you hate."

"We'll take D— with us."

"Or you could come here and live with me."

Justin was always a step ahead of me in the thinking game, or maybe I just wasn't as good of a planner as him. It was true that I didn't totally hate Miskwi even though I had once thought I did. But that had been before I met Justin and it's amazing how happiness changes your opinion of so many things that aren't related to its source. Justin convinced me how easy it would be to walk into the child welfare office myself and say, "For the same reasons you took my brother away, I need to be out of that house too," and then ask to live with Justin and his mother. Glory wasn't too excited by the idea of fostering me, at least not until Justin reminded her that I had lots of experience taking care of my sick brother.

"Could D— come live here too?"

"Not enough room, sexy, but you could see him as much as you see him now."

"I don't know. I want to do something more exciting."

"Like what? Want me to eat your family? Yum, a plump little boy!" Justin laughed at his words, but I did not think they were any laughing matter.

"You're not serious about any of this are you?"

"I am, I am. I just don't know what you want to do. You're all over the place with plans and stuff, and I'm just waiting for you to make up your mind."

"Fine."

Glory called out that it was time to drive me home, and I made it loud and clear to Justin when I left that he had really upset me. I didn't kiss him goodbye, I didn't say goodbye, and I didn't say I'd meet him in WolfDen later that night. I didn't say a word to Glory on the drive home either, not even to ask her to roll down the car window so I didn't have to suffer the bad side effects of her filthy habit. Every time I came back from Justin's my mother accused me of smoking, and every time I told her that she could check my pockets all she wanted because it wasn't me it was my stupid friends. I wonder why she never asked about my stupid friends. You would think if a mother was concerned about her child being peer-pressured into bad habits that she'd want to get to the root of the problem. Then again, I think she knew that I was telling the truth about not smoking and so by not asking me about my stupid friends she was just being wise about not creating a situation where I'd have to lie.

Anyway, I got home that night and had supper with my family, and then I went to my room and did homework until I couldn't stop myself from logging onto WolfDen. Justin had been right that I needed to make up my mind and so I needed to apologize and be direct with him from then on. Remember how I said that sometimes when an idea pops into your head it grows and expands until it's all you can think about? I mean it is *all* you can think about and you absolutely have to do something about it, like either act on it or put it totally out of your head or else you'll go insane like those guys in the Miskwi House of Corrections who realize too late. Well, I had to act. To make sure I was truly ready, I thought considerably about it before logging onto WolfDen and came up with these facts: I did not want to be like any of the other M—'s and I did not want to be like H—. In fact I didn't want to be like anybody from Miskwi, and the only way that was going to happen was if I took my life into my own hands and made plans and decisions for my best interest, which my parents—the people who were supposed to make sure I had the best life possible and definitely better than theirs ever was—hadn't done. I thought about it some more and decided that Justin's mother had failed him in that way too even though she liked to brag about how she had raised him single-handedly and protected him from the "revolving door of relationship tragedy". That was total BS, because what Glory had done in reality was keep Justin to herself and make it publicly known by honking her horn at him every day after work that he belonged to her in a featureless gray portable like her slave in a closet. I thought about D—, about how no matter where he was in life there would always be people who made fun of him, and if he didn't have my father to crack them in the jaw then who would he have? Finally I thought about Dargelos from that book, the way him and the other characters did what they wanted and had their own little society that protected them from grown-ups trying to control and prevent what they did. I have to say, that night was my defining moment, the night I became true to myself and did what was best for *me*, which nobody had ever done, not even Justin, really, even though I still love him with all my heart.

runawaybitch13 (9:06 pm):
u there?

Dargelos23 (9:06 pm):
yeah

runawaybitch13 (9:06 pm):
sorry we had a fight 2day

Dargelos23 (9:06 pm):
we did?

runawaybitch13 (9:07 pm):
didnt we?

Dargelos23 (9:07 pm):
i guess. im sorry 2

runawaybitch13 (9:07 pm):
when ur, u know, a werewolf r u dangerous?

Dargelos23 (9:07 pm):
can b. why?

runawaybitch13 (9:08 pm):
how much longer will u b 1?

Dargelos23 (9:08 pm):
dunno, not long. im starting 2 feel better

runawaybitch13 (9:08 pm):
but ur still 1 now right?

Dargelos23 (9:08 pm):
grrrrowl lol!

runawaybitch13 (9:09 pm):
so i have a plan: it begins with us killing my parents and ends with me living with u

Man convicted of slaying girlfriend's family in Miskwi

by *The Miskwi Sun* December 6, 2008

Today the Superior Court found 25-year-old Justin Stein guilty on three counts of first-degree murder of a Miskwi family. This brings to an end the most appalling and bizarre tragedy in the town's history.

The bodies of Mr. and Mrs. Richards and their eight-year-old son, who suffered from Down syndrome, were discovered brutally slain in the family's residence on the morning of April 23, 2006.

Mr. Richards suffered 24 stab wounds and pathologists believe he fought hard for his life. Mrs. Richards suffered 12 stab wounds, and the boy's neck was slit open from ear to ear.

Crime scene evidence suggested that Stein and the Richards' 13-year-old daughter engaged in sexual intercourse on the Richards' bed after the massacre. When questioned, Stein blushed and looked away. The juvenile claimed she was a virgin despite contradictory medical evidence.

Stein will be sentenced in the upcoming days to life in prison without parole. The juvenile, now 15, will be the first in the country to face the maximum youth sentence of 10 years. She will serve 4 years in detention and the remaining 6 in a highly structured program within the community. Her identity is protected under the Youth Act.

According to Stein, the juvenile asked him to kill her parents. He claimed they threatened to report him to the police for statutory rape, locked the juvenile in her bedroom regularly, and subjected her to psychological and physical abuse.

The juvenile said she did not think Stein would actually kill her parents. She claimed that after he stabbed them, Stein threatened her with the same knife and ordered her to slit her eight-year-old brother's throat to save her own life. Stein denied this allegation and declared his love for the juvenile today in court.

"We haven't seen each other in two years but it's like we're engaged. We're soulmates, and I'm going to marry her in a German castle some day."

Stein believes he is a 300-year-old werewolf. He used to wear vials of blood around his neck.

"I don't know what was in them," mother Glory Stein told one reporter. "My son is a sweet, gentle-natured boy."

According to a witness who works at the department store where Stein used to work, Stein and the juvenile started dating about two months before the massacre.

"Justin seemed like such a normal guy. I knew M— from school and she was always a little weird, like, into dark things. She wasn't mean, exactly, but she wasn't nice unless she wanted something from you."

Stein and the juvenile met regularly in public, but nobody questioned the inappropriate nature of the relationship. They were members of an Internet website called WolfDen, where it is believed they planned the Richards family massacre.

The juvenile has been detained in a psychiatric hospital south of Miskwi since April 24, 2006. She has responded well to treatment and discovered a love for storytelling. She has expressed desire to become a counselor for children with special needs. She faces sentencing next week.

BLEARY

Bleary. The name says it all: Bleary Center for Today's Youth. Well okay, the name doesn't say it all if you take it at face value. What kind of youth, for example? And what about the fact that it isn't so much a center for today's youth at-large as a live-in facility for those without proper families? Some with criminal records, even. No, I'm talking about the isolated word *bleary*. Anybody who has a mind to look up its meaning in a dictionary will learn it stands for blurriness or vagueness, but if you consider the word some more it sounds like a hybrid of *bleak* and *weary*. That's how the name says it all.

I was part of the first round of teens sent to live in the Alberta youth correctional facility. The Bleary Project, as the government referred to it in the beginning to win public support, was launched to help misguided youth, to teach them better ways so they could become productive members of society. The project was only possible because some wealthy old man died alone in his bed one night and left behind a Will that designated his estate to a worthy cause. Why Mr. Bleary never did it when he was alive, with all that that money he had, perplexes me to this day.

So the Bleary Project was launched and within months there was a waiting list of parents who wanted to enroll their children. Parents from all over Canada, the project had gained such rapid popularity. Kids from outside provinces were eligible to be admitted into the home, but they had to be suffering—or rather, their parents had to be—under what were called "special circumstances". After some dramatic convincing on my mother's part, my parents were deemed eligible and I became the first Quebec kid living under the most special circumstances.

"You'll get a great education there," my mother said, after she and my father made the announcement on the breakfast of my seventeenth birthday. "They have special courses that aren't taught in regular high schools, and you'll get to wear a handsome uniform."

Parents don't seem to realize that the words "special" and "uniform" translate in their kids' minds to "Loser" and "Hell" respectively.

"And there are lots of bears out there," my father added lamely.

"Bears? For heaven's sake, Nathaniel, why would he look forward to bears?"

You would have thought I was being sent away to a summer camp or something, the way my mother suddenly became concerned about my safety. She hadn't been so concerned about it the week before when I lit the neighbor's garbage can on fire and caught the tail of my father's smoking jacket, too—I sometimes enjoyed being dressed up for these occasions. One of my slower nights that one was, and my negligence in wearing loose clothing while setting trash cans afire, well, pretty much nipped it in the bud. And I suppose the fact that I merely removed my father's jacket and dropped it into the flames would be why my mother wasn't concerned about my safety.

"I bought your father that jacket our first year together," she said, as soon as the cops left our home. "He's had that jacket for nineteen years."

"Then it's time for a new one," I yawned, stretching against my great-great grandfather's high-backed mahogany chair while my mother paced the living room and tugged at her fingertips as though trying to remove a pair of fitted gloves.

"Oh mercy!" she wailed to the gathering of fat naked ladies painted onto the living room's dome ceiling. "What have I done to deserve a son like this?"

"Must have been pretty bad," I said, in my gravest voice, the same one my father used whenever he (or so I thought in my younger years) made an intelligent remark about the state of the world.

"Trigger. To your bedroom."

Trigger. Yes, that's my name. The same word you use to identify on which part of a gun one person presses his finger to shoot another. Oh, the names they called me in elementary school: Cowgirl, Horse Monger. Other boys didn't like me because they thought I was a sissy, especially by grade five when my hair was long enough to tie in a ponytail, and girls wouldn't have anything to do with me because they thought I had an unhealthy attraction to horses. In high school the names got worse: Trashy White Nigger, Jew Killer, Wife Beater (though that one gave me hope—if they were willing to call me Wife Beater then it meant they thought I was capable of getting myself one someday, whom I would never beat, of course). Basically, if the word rhymed with my name while simultaneously insulting a type of person, I was labeled with it.

Back to these bears my father seemed to think I would like so much in Alberta. It was my turn to ask him, with all my male casualness, "What the hell do I care about bears?" See, I wasn't quite afraid of them (I had never had an encounter with one so how could I judge?), but I had always felt more at ease around animals that could be tied to fenceposts.

Many times when I trespassed people's properties to steal their garbage or set it on fire, I had to deal with anything from yappers to deep-bellied barkers. Once or twice I got bit, though nothing too serious, but most times the dogs liked me just fine and were pleased with my peace offerings of ham hocks fresh from the butcher's that day. One time I even brought a dog home with me, he looked so unkempt. His fur was missing in patches, and his left eye was sealed shut with a layer of gluey yellow. My heart went out to him.

"What are you doing with the Wickers' dog?" my mother demanded, as I carried the poor animal in my arms. He was a good-sized thing, a border collie I seem to remember, and I was having some difficulty getting him up the spiral stairs to my bedroom with discretion. I placed him gingerly on one of the steps and leaned over the banister to confront my mother.

"He's been abused. We need to get him to a vet."

My mother gaped up at me from the foyer. Her head was cranked back, and her eyes were so wide that from my perspective she looked like one of those mock-classy cartoon ladies ironed onto the T-shirts that blue-collar men wear proudly on weekends while they mow their lawns and rake leaves and their beer bellies expand over their imitation designer workpants from Walmart. "*Pasha* has cancer."

"Well then he really needs a vet," I persisted, not letting myself think too much about why he was really missing patches of fur, then.

My mother rubbed the sides of her head the way she did whenever the world became too much for her. "Where did you find him?"

"I found him wandering the streets." I glanced over my shoulder for a little support from Pasha, but Pasha had resigned to his spot on the step and dozed off.

"Nathaniel, call the police."

"No. Mom, wait. Please. I didn't set anything on fire. I swear!"

And that was the final straw. The one that made my mother decide to ship me off to Bleary. She had been doing research for some months before, looking into and even visiting private youth facilities in the Montreal area, but as long as they were on streets where trashcans were deposited on street curbs twice per week, she kept looking.

Why, you might be asking yourself, did I light people's garbage on fire? And who on earth would risk trespassing on another person's property simply to steal their discards? But if you consider the act, I was doing them a favor.

I was no pyromaniac, but I had always been mesmerized by fire. It had so many good uses. The house I grew up in had a great big maroon brick fireplace in the living room and a smaller tiled exterior one in my parents' bedroom. I used to love spreading myself across my parents' bed when their fireplace was lit, especially at night when I could gaze up at the skylight and see the reflection of the soft orange flames engaging in a sort of visual symphony with the stars. During these times, my mind would drift into that lucid state where we become capable of thoughts there aren't time for in the day-to-day rush of things.

On one of those nights, when I was maybe thirteen or fourteen, the view beyond the skylight reminded me of these two homeless men I had seen huddled over a trashcan bonfire on my way home from school that day. Even though they were dressed in rags and their hands and faces were smeared in dirt that would eventually become part of their natural skin tones, they seemed content. And instead of asking passers-by for spare change or a bite of their sandwiches, the two men asked, very politely, for bits and scraps of paper or cardboard.

They asked one woman who lit her last cigarette if they could have the empty pack. They asked a businessman about to chuck the *Gazette* away if he would mind giving it to them. I figured they were going to throw the paper into the flames, but they did something far more admirable: the two homeless men divided its contents between them and read, exchanged their sections and read some more. Then they shared a brief conversation about the tensions in the Middle East and how Canada was independent enough to resist a possible U.S. recession, and *then* they tossed the paper into the fire.

Fire was keeping these men in touch with the world and warm under its depressive chill. It gave them light I was certain God could never compete with.

After that I guess you could say I became obsessed with fire. It gave me light, too. I took to the habit of stealing garbage and bringing it to the homeless, or lighting trashcan contents on fire right where I found them. Especially in the neighborhood where I grew up, everybody was so rich the items they threw away could keep the entire city lit for a week! Try explaining this to your parents, though, and their friends who all happened to live in the same neighborhood. To them I was a pyromaniac. My mother even called in a renovation company to seal off our two fireplaces, and then she called in an alarm company to install a sprinkler in the ceiling of every room except our two bathrooms and the basement laundry room. Everybody waited for me to set those off purely because I could, but I never entertained the idea.

My best Bleary memory is actually the first time I saw Alberta. I hated Alberta in the beginning, especially because I arrived in winter, which was severe and inescapable because I couldn't seek refuge by the fireplace in my parents' bedroom. But compared to my entire Bleary experience, I guess beggars can't be choosers.

Because it was winter, I saw nothing but white. White land that loped along for miles, white-glazed trees, white-capped mountains with navy blue bodies that looked like upside-down snow cones. And while it was as cold as Montreal on that particular day, the cold was fresh. The air felt as pure as pure spring water, the kind that seems to evaporate in your mouth. The wind didn't cut but rather grazed your skin courteously, and it carried with it the scent of pine and, well, health, if health has an odor. In the following weeks I would learn how Albertans live in harmony with nature, inviting it into their backyards to nurse on saplings, slowing their vehicles to allow pedestrian mammals the right-of-way, yawning with the sun over an herbal tea at dawn. When I first arrived in Alberta, though, I was not prepared for this drastic change in lifestyle.

"You told me I would like it here," I accused my mother over the phone. She had told me (which makes me think I must have wanted to get away from her as much as she wanted me away) that I might even like it out in Alberta so much I wouldn't want to come home once I was of legal age.

"Trigger," she crackled through the line, "Bleary is a correctional facility. I said you would find it beneficial not fun."

"Where's dad?"

"Watching the news."

"Oh yeah?" I felt infused with rage toward my father, who had played no evident part in any of the major decisions about my life lately. "Tell him to tune in for the six o'clock tomorrow. There's going to be a nice forest fire somewhere in Alberta." Then I slammed down the receiver and stomped to the top floor of the Bleary Center to find my bedroom.

The place was small and polite like a basket of handpicked berries, but you have to understand I was used to large impersonal spaces and color schemes that made you feel like the large impersonal spaces were closing in on you. The two-story ranch house was shared between eight kids and alternating staff members, and space was so limited everybody lived on top of everybody else. There were five bedrooms upstairs, and they were all very much the same. Mine was at the end of the hallway farthest from the staircase, across from the bathroom. Each bedroom had two single beds, matching night tables and dressers, roomy closets, and a bay window that took up almost an entire wall. The girls' rooms were painted in summer colors and the boys' in fall ones, and every bedroom was adorned with Canadian wildlife knickknacks like beaver bookends and moose antler wall racks. At the time I was too rife with contempt to have an opinion. Now I think, that's a sure way to breed hostility. Making fun of kids by giving them Ken and Barbie bedrooms in the middle of nowhere in a juvenile Alcatraz.

In my bedroom that first day at Bleary there was also another guy, and I was in no mood for company. In fact I had assumed I would have a private room since my mother was shelling out precious charity funds to secure me a place there. I stopped at the bedroom entrance and glared at the intruder, who was lying on one of the beds, arms tucked lazily behind his head, a half-smoked cigarette dangling from his mouth. I had never smoked a cigarette and, despite my tendencies, had no interest in trying.

"So you're the New Boy," drawled the intruder.

"Please put out your cigarette."

"Nah. I was just leaving." The intruder swung his legs over the side of the bed and was deftly walking towards me. He hadn't looked so tall while he was lying down.

"Derrick," he said. He lifted an arm above his head and made a fist. I stepped back and gave him a wide berth to exit the room. I had never known of the knuckle high-five before then, and so I thought maybe Derrick was about to land me a blow on the head—that's what kids in "The System" did was all I had ever heard before I arrived at Bleary.

"Trigger."

Derrick coughed on his next cigarette inhalation, and I hardened. "Got a problem?"

"Nah, man. Trigger, eh?"

"Yeah?"

"We should shoot pool sometime."

Well. As you can imagine, I thought this was some sort of joke. Or perhaps a ploy. Something my mother had orchestrated so as to ensure I would be miserable during my stay at the Bleary Center. When I confronted the social workers there that day, a man and a woman in their late twenties, both bundled in dark green hand-knit sweaters with deer heads embroidered on the sleeves, they reacted very calmly and assured me this had nothing to do with my mother.

"Derrick doesn't live here," Anna, the woman social worker, sighed. "He did for a while, but now he's out on probation. He likes to come around though, likes the food here. "

I raised my eyebrows. I mean I was no food critic or anything, but how good could whatever they served at Bleary possibly be? Frank, the male social worker, tapped Anna on the arm and then the two of them disappeared into the staff office, adjacent to the kitchen. Frank closed the door as quietly as could be so as not to make me feel excluded I guess, my first day there. That's when Avril, yet another social worker, burst through the front door and presented herself before me like she might have been one of the kids living there, she looked so flushed and excited.

"Anna? Frank? Why is Derrick outside?"

I had never been one to stick my hand out for a shake when I met somebody new, even though it was a manner my mother was always trying to instill in me, but something about Avril, something about her neat dress pants and crisp blouse, summoned that gesture from me.

"Trigger. I'm the new kid. For now."

"Oh! For now?" Avril placed her handbag on the floor between her feet (she was wearing standard black dress shoes with just enough of a heel to let people know she was a serious woman but not a dictator). Her arm extended on impulse, but then I hesitated and so we stood facing each other in a kind of beguiled state.

"Or maybe for good. I think that's what they're talking about right now." I nodded at the closed office door and shrugged a lot more nonchalantly than I felt.

Avril pointed to the office door. "Who? What are they talking about?"

"Never mind." I took one step to the left and walked past Avril, who took one step to the side herself so I had ample space, and as I passed her I felt the tips of her fingers on my shoulder like a sprinkle of water from a tree that's still wet from a recent rainfall and has its leaves turned upside-down by a rush of wind.

I was on probation my first week at Bleary. That meant I wasn't allowed to stay out until nine o'clock at night like the rest of the kids, and naturally that made me the laughingstock of the house. Since I didn't have a roommate, I was missing out on the bonding experiences shared by the other kids, who all shared bedrooms, and at dinnertime I was left out of their conversations, ignored even. Anna and Frank tried to include me by telling the other kids I had come from one of Canada's most exciting cities, but since they had never been there themselves, their ignorance more or less made a mockery out of me. My sixth night there, while the other kids engaged in a unanimous rant about another who had left a few days before my arrival (he had been sent to a stricter facility in British Columbia where he was to await sentencing), Avril sat beside me at the dinner table and asked about my parents.

"Later," I whispered. Why on earth would she ask about my parents in front of a bunch of people who had no respect for me already? The last thing I needed was to appear like a Momma's Boy.

"I mean," Avril corrected, "what do they do? Jamie's mother is a paralegal, Shawn's father builds aircraft engines, and Tamara's father works in the oil industry."

I surveyed the table and saw that none of the other kids seemed to have heard Avril's question, or at least if they had they didn't seem interested in my answer. Jamie was busy making flapping gestures with his arms as he recounted a near-death experience he had had one time with Brent (the kid who had been sent away); Shawn was trying to compete with his own tales of out-of-body experience (which to me sounded bogus and suspiciously like somebody else's story, maybe belonging to a pilot he had met at his father's aircraft company); and Tamara and the others were satisfied being a captive audience.

I turned my chair sideways so I was facing Avril. "My father's a university professor and my mother's a charity whore."

"Trigger!"

"That's what she calls herself."

"In public?"

"No, but she does to her friends and frankly she should call herself that all the time. Mrs. Derringer, Charity Whore."

Avril stared at me, I had shocked her that much. I hadn't meant to, and right as I started to apologize she set loose a stream of hiccup sounds and brought a hand to her mouth, which seemed to open and close involuntarily. The dinner table fell quiet.

Frank asked, "Are you okay, Avril?"

Anna asked, "Avril, what is it?"

Both looked worriedly from Avril to me, and then back to Avril, who by that point had leaned forward and pressed her forehead to the table. The table wobbled in rhythm with her hiccups, which had graduated to one of the most beautiful God-given sounds a person can make: laughter.

"I'm sorry, everybody," Avril said, as she straightened herself out and pushed away from the table. Her face was pink, and her eyes danced like the fire and stars did in my parents' skylight. "Trigger was just, he was just telling me about his parents. His mother especially." Avril glanced my way and winked. Or rather, blinked the wetness from her eyes so as not to further alarm her co-workers, but I knew there was also a secret wink in there for me.

The next day after I returned from school I found the house empty except for Anna. She unlocked the front door with one hand while she held a cookie tray in the other. Her hair was wrapped around her head in a wreath of wiry salt and pepper and pinned at the top with a falcon clip, and I had to fight the urge to ask if she ever tired of Canadian wildlife. I was about to head upstairs and start my homework, for what else could I do within the parameters of my probation since I wasn't allowed more than fifty meters from the center and the closest town with anything to do was a mile away, but Anna poked a finger at the ceiling and smiled.

"Congratulations, Trigger."

"Eh?"

"Today at our staff meeting, we decided to remove your probation conditions."

"Okay." Anna's enthusiasm was not infecting me the way I imagine she had hoped it would. I could tell because as long as I stood there waiting for her to elaborate, her presumptuous eyes darkened and her mouth puckered inward.

"We decided, *Avril* decided, you should start with a clean slate. Normally kids here have to *earn* privileges."

"I just got here, and I haven't done anything wrong, so I agree with Avril."

"You're a fire-starter, Trigger. No, actually, you're old enough now to be considered a pyromaniac."

Whoa, the accusations! I could not help but become very tall and rigid, like I had expanded into a stone statue in front of Anna. Anna took a step backward and placed both hands on her cookie tray and raised it to her chest.

"Can I go out now?"

Anna craned her head sideways to look at her watch. Her hands held firmly to the cookie tray. "Will you be home for supper? We're having cold-cut sandwiches."

"And cookies."

"What?"

I pointed to the tray.

"Yes, and cookies."

"I think I'll pass." I turned to head upstairs to change out of my school uniform, and Anna turned to go back to her dinner preparations, and then I asked, "When is Avril coming in?"

Anna continued walking away as she answered, "Tomorrow."

I hadn't yet been into town, but the school bus drove through it so I knew it was a straight walk along Main Street from the Bleary Center. A brisk, chilly walk at that, as I hadn't yet been provided with Alberta-appropriate outerwear. I jogged the distance to town impressively fast for a boy who had just a week before lived in a major city where public transportation was available from one street corner to the next, so the first thing I decided to do once I arrived in town was treat myself to a hot sausage roll at Jack's Deli. The entire deli was probably the size of the family room in my parents' house—a flaking melamine service counter long enough to seat six, behind which the cook and waitress shared workspace, three tables for four along the windowed wall, a jukebox in the far corner beside which was the door to the bathroom, and a full-sized pool table at the center of the deli. The pool table was worth more than the deli, probably. Its dark wood base shone penny-new and the red felt surface looked perfectly unused, like a magazine ad, the way the brand-new balls were arranged in a flawless triangle, two pool cues lined up neatly beside.

Once my order was ready, I sat at one of the tables by the window and leafed through the daily somebody before me had left behind. The first page covered national news, and when I read about Montreal's upcoming winter festival I was surprised to feel a nip of homesickness. Otherwise, Alberta litanies about wheat and oil and livestock held no value to me.

"Come here to shoot pool or shoot the shit?"

I looked up and there he was, Derrick, leaning against the pool table with one chapped Kodiak boot crossed over the other, laces undone, jeans stuffed inside the tops.

"Shoot the what?"

"Shoot the shit. That's what the old men do when they come here, read the daily then shoot the shit like theys all informed about the world. Ain't nothing to know about the world that I don't already know."

Derrick spoke in a lazy, drawling tongue that suited his poor English. If anything I suspected he had said "theys" and "ain't" on purpose, a way of asserting himself, maybe even of testing me. Derrick struck me as somebody who regularly tested people. It showed in his posture, the way he didn't scrunch up like everybody does when they stand for too long (especially in a diner with cardboard-thin walls and without central heat), the way he rocked forward onto the balls of his feet to add a little height.

"I'll be honest with you, Derrick, I've never *shot* pool before."

"Where you from?" Derrick jutted his hips back and pushed off the pool table. He sat across from me, and I noticed that the skin of his face was slightly discolored and patchy, like maybe he had a faint birthmark that covered most of the front and continued around his head and down his neck. One eye was more sunken than the other and a little lazy to the outside.

"Montreal. Montreal, Quebec. Other side of Canada." It wasn't that I thought Derrick was ignorant, but something about him in that moment seemed vulnerable, maybe volatile. Or maybe I was projecting and I just wanted a friend for once, and I sensed that to earn Derrick's friendship would require a degree of precision on my part.

"Oh yeah, I been there. Real good cod and lobster."

So it turned out Derrick didn't know, yet I admired his confidence.

We shot the shit for a while longer before I had to regretfully inform Derrick I had a curfew. It pleased me when he nodded thoughtfully and reminisced about his time at Bleary.

"There was this one lady that was real tight with me, even let me stay out late sometimes. Avery. You met her yet?"

"Sure." I said so casually, for I didn't want to let on Avril was the reason I was allowed out that evening. I had told Derrick I was sent to Bleary because of marriage troubles between my parents, told him my parents were wealthy enough to pay for me to be in a more ideal situation while they worked out their relationship kinks.

"They send any of that wealth here with you?"

"Sure," I lied. "I get a bigger allowance than the others, but don't tell anybody. Don't want any fights starting or anything."

"Who'd I tell? Only had one friend there if you count Ariel."

We rose from the table and once again Derrick dangled his arm over his head and made a fist with his hand. "High-five, man."

Even though I knew by now this was Derrick's way of telling me I was his kind, I was "in", I paused before touching my knuckles to his. He sensed my hesitation.

"Yeah, man. That's the way to do it. Like this." He raised his other arm. I met my knuckles to his again and was rewarded with a great big decaying grin. The cook and the waitress behind the service counter eyed us disapprovingly, but Derrick paid them no attention. Outside the deli, he gave a rather careless wave considering how excited he had been just seconds before and then bolted up Main Street opposite my direction, the impact from his Kodiaks making cracks in the sidewalk ice.

On my way back to Bleary, I stopped at a convenience store that sold pre-arranged bouquets of flowers and bought one for Avril / Avery / Ariel. I would tell Anna the bouquet was for the home, a centerpiece for the dining room table, and the next morning I would mention to Avril that she had been on my mind when I bought it—because she had been able to have my probation conditions removed. Avril was flattered when I told her the next morning, and she even blushed when I suggested she put the flower vase in her office, where the flowers would have a better chance of surviving since there was a bay window. Every damn room at Bleary had a bay window, but I wanted there to be a way for Avril to privately acknowledge my gift.

"That's very nice of you, Trigger. Well! Your mother should be proud of such a thoughtful son."

"I think the flowers would look especially nice on the windowsill."

"You know, I think they work best here on the table. They're so pretty, and I wouldn't want to keep that all to myself. But thank you, Trigger."

I had grown to really respect Avril. Compared with the other Bleary social workers she showed an interest in me, in my "special circumstances". She had this proud, wounded air about her that made her at once stern and human. Even though I had no prior experience with "The System", I knew from other kids at my high school that social workers didn't go into the field because they loved youth or even wanted to help them. Well maybe they did love the kids they worked with, but that love came from a place of hate. Pure, unmitigated anger for the years of abuse and neglect they had suffered as children. Avril never confided any of her childhood traumas to me, but we did once have this conversation that gave me a better sense of who she was.

It was maybe my third or fourth month at Bleary, and none of the other kids were home; they had gone on a hiking trip with Frank and a group of volunteer students from some local university, and I had refused to go because I thought any and all people affiliated with universities were jelly-boned like my father. Anna was out on an errand, and so I was helping Avril prepare supper. She looked especially tired that evening considering she had had the weekend off.

"Actually, I didn't," she said, when I joked that her weekend must have been so casual she forgot to dress properly for work that day (she usually wore gray slacks and a starchy rose or teal blouse, whereas that day she was in cargos and a turtleneck without personality).

"Then it must be casual Monday," I said.

Avril opened the oven and inserted a tray of easy-bake croissants, something she did special for me every so often since Alberta didn't otherwise have good croissants like back home. "I had to work on a case, that's all."

"Oh." I knew that conversation was over. "So, hey, why don't you guys take Derrick in?" I had been wanting to ask that question for a long time. I had even made up my mind to offer half of my bedroom.

"What do you mean, Trigger? We really don't like Derrick being around the house so much."

"Why not? It's not like his is something to brag about. That crazy father of his and all."

Avril let go of the oven door and it slapped shut. "What did you say?"

"Nothing." Now that I had Avril's full attention, I didn't want it. Her face took on this expression like either she wanted to cry about something she had done that nobody else knew about, or she wanted to walk out the back door and keep walking until she disappeared into the mountains. When she next spoke, it was like some vicious part of her was talking to me, that part that comes from a place of hate.

"You cannot—*cannot* go to Derrick's house anymore, Trigger. Do you understand?"

"Sure."

"Do you understand?

"It's not like I go there all the time. He lives far and all that's nearby is a lame graveyard."

"Trigger, it's one thing that Derrick shows up looking for food. That's okay, we try to feed him because we know his family is poor. But he's trouble and he comes around looking for that, too."

"What kind of trouble?"

"He's done some serious things, and I disagree with his probation. And he's not supposed to be on the premises."

"Then why doesn't anybody stop him? You keep feeding a stray dog and he'll keep coming around. I know he did some bad things, but none of it was his fault. He told me. It's that crazy father of his. He'd make any person want to do bad things."

Avril crumpled onto a kitchen chair and smacked her hands over her face. I knew she was determined to hold the tears in by the way she was pressing her palms to the crests of her cheeks like she was trying to hold something broken together.

"What, Avril? What is it? Did he ever hurt you?" If that were the case, I would have to reassess Derrick.

"No." Avril's hands dropped away, and I saw how twisted her face was with exhaustion and apology. Her voice sounded small, uncertain. "You cannot go to Derrick's house anymore. You've got intelligence, Trigger. Use it."

Avril excused herself into the staff office and left me standing there by the stove like just another problem youth. I had been having an earnest conversation with her one moment and then cast away the next, surely categorized in her mind with the lot of other youth she didn't approve of for this reason or that. And what had I done wrong, exactly? I hadn't been told flat-out by her or any other Bleary worker that I was forbidden to spend time at Derrick's house, and now suddenly it was off limits with a strict punishing finger wagging over my head. Fuck that, I was going to Derrick's.

Avril was busy locked in her office, so I was able to freely walk out of the house. I did so out the back door, as a matter of fact, walked right past the office window and waved. I realize this was a mean thing to do because Avril had just been trying to help me, but at that particular moment she was no better than my mother all the way back in Montreal with her sealed up, Trigger-proof fireplaces. I needed something to dim the bright anger that had suddenly manifested itself. I needed something more than Derrick, and I needed it right then. So on the way to Derrick's, I stopped at the only liquor store I had learned about in the area and bought the cheapest bottle of wine there. The store clerk asked me how old I was, and I said nineteen. He examined me and asked if I wasn't one of the Bleary kids and I replied, "*Mais non*, I'm from Montreal, here visiting a friend. Derrick. Derrick Holmes."

The clerk didn't register recognition when I said Derrick's full name, but he was impressed with my French. "I was in Montreal once. Lots of pretty girls there." He rang up my wine and gave me my change, and then I strode out of the store and right to Derrick's front door, which was wide open to expose a blister of discarded needles and empty beer bottles right at the entrance.

"Rick!" A man somewhere in his late thirties hollered for Derrick after I took the liberty of walking into the house and peering inside the living room. Three additional men slouched on threadbare easy chairs, each tightening an elastic band around his biceps by pulling on the band with his teeth, then smacking his forearm with the opposite hand, and then groaning with unrestrained pleasure when the needle pierced his skin. A choir of junkies. A scrappy Heinz fifty-seven padded into the living room and gazed up at me. His eyes were overcast with cataracts and his nostrils clogged with snot. I went to pat him on the head, remembering poor old Pasha, but then the man who had hollered for Derrick aimed his foot at the dog's barrel and sent the animal flying and yelping into the hallway. The dog landed on his side and made a hacking sound and then gurgled vomit all over the floor. I had to cover my nose and mouth, it smelled so foul.

"Goddamn smells like shit. Eat it, mutt." The dog whined and the man yelled at him. "I said eat it!"

I never felt so disgusted as when the dog lowered his head and began to lick the floor.

"Hey, man, didn't know you were coming." Derrick's slap on my shoulder was my ticket out. As much as I wanted to escape the scene and these men who hadn't been there the other times I visited (nobody but Derrick had been there), I knew better than to say it out loud, to even let it show in my expression.

"Pa?"

The man who had hollered for Derrick, it turned out, was his father. I'd never met his father even though I had told Avril differently, just heard all kinds of stories about him from Derrick. Not one had prepared me for the actual man.

"What? You and your little bitch want some junk? She's too young for that shit. You're gonna dry her up before she can push a baby out."

"No, Pa. We're gonna take a walk, have a drink in the graveyard. Any beer left?"

Derrick's father rubbed his hands up and down his face and split open a cut on one of his cheeks. When he stopped rubbing his face there were red skid marks all over it, but he didn't seem concerned or even to notice. He swayed as he stood in place, and if he had told Derrick there was no beer left I would have guessed he'd recently finished it himself.

"There's a forty-ouncer in the bathtub. Shit stuff. Whale piss."

Derrick nodded emphatically and then galloped upstairs. I followed.

I turned the hallway corner to his bedroom and was greeted by a girl who introduced herself as Cassy, the girlfriend whom Derrick had spoken of many times but I had yet to meet. She lay sprawled across the bed on her back, strands of dark brown hair parachuting over the edge.

"Hey. I'm Trigger."

Suddenly Cassy was upright and staring at me like I was a rock star. Her face turned scarlet from sitting up so quickly, and I wondered how old she really was. Derrick had told me fifteen but she looked more like eleven or twelve, mostly because her cheeks jiggled with the kind of fat that should melt away with puberty. "I've heard *so* much about you! Derrick talks about you all the time! It's always like 'Trigger this' and 'Trigger that' and if he wasn't so in love with me I'd say he's gay for you!"

Derrick marched into the room with an unopened forty-ounce of Fire and Ice beer. He held it up like a trophy even though his father had called it whale piss. I myself had little experience with beer. In fact I had barely acquired a taste for wine like the kind I had picked up at the liquor store before.

Cassy clapped her hands together and squealed. "Let's get drunk!"

"You're already there, babe. Let's walk it off before we start on this."

I was surprised by the way Derrick sat beside Cassy and hooked an arm around her shoulders as gently as he did. I was even more surprised when he kissed her on the cheek and whispered, "I love you," into her ear.

He turned to me and asked, "Want to do whippets before we go?"

"Go where?"

"The graveyard."

Cassy giggled delightedly. "The graveyard! The graveyard!" She propelled herself backward and was once again sprawled across the bed. The T-shirt she was wearing rode upward to expose a pale, freckled, formless midriff, and I knew she was not fifteen.

"What are whippets?" I asked.

"My friend," began Derrick, ducking under his bed to retrieve a backpack, "you must have a whippet to know what a whippet is." He sorted through the backpack and produced three unused party balloons, a baggy containing white powder, and a silver spray can. "Now watch."

He handed a balloon to Cassy, who took it expectantly and blew into it. When the balloon was near full, she pinched the opening shut with her thumb and index finger and beamed up at Derrick. "Okay, Cassy baby, just open it a tiny bit."

Cassy complied eagerly and released her hold on the balloon opening so Derrick could pour white powder inside. "Maybe not that much, D-Rock. He might get sick."

Derrick considered his girlfriend's caution and looked to me. "You wanna get buzzed or like really, really in the zone?"

Truth was, I had no experience with drugs except the few joints Derrick had shared with me. Even then I had pretended to inhale, had even managed to imitate the cough Derrick made when he took an especially deep inhalation. "Buzzed—to start."

"Good choice, man. Smart."

Next Derrick shook the can, inserted the nozzle into the balloon and sprayed. Cassy clamped the balloon shut with her fingers and shook it like a box of raffle tickets. Derrick nodded approvingly and then decided to shake the balloon once himself to make sure everything was mixed properly. The pair worked together like experts.

"Okay," he instructed, "hold it shut until the tip is in your mouth and then let go. Just let go and take in as much as you can. It won't hurt like weed, but you wanna take in as much as you can to get the best high. Okay? Ready?"

"What's going to happen?"

"You'll get high."

"What kind of high?"

"The good kind. I promise."

Next I remember we were in the graveyard, which was quite a walk from Derrick's house, but that night walking was no trouble for us. I wasn't convinced I was high at first, after Derrick and Cassy did their whippets and we left the house, but they both assured me that I was as high as a suicide bomber and all the good feelings I was experiencing were because of my whippet. Wonderful whippets. It had grown dark, very dark, certainly past my curfew, but I'd gained the trust of not only Avril but also Frank and even Anna so how severely could they punish me for coming home late just that once? Not to mention it was Friday night and other boys my age and some younger were allowed out past nine. Or was it Saturday night? Or was it a weekday?

"Shit."

"What, Trigger?" Cassy had developed nervous tendencies since her whippet. Her head tipped from left to right in jerky spasms, and saliva coated the outside of her mouth no matter that she licked it up every few seconds.

"What day is it?"

"Tuesday?"

"Really? Shit."

"I dunno. Derrick baby, what day is it?"

"Dunno. It's a new day now. Gotta be past midnight."

"Shit."

We had settled ourselves along a row of tombstones that were flush with the ground, old, unreadable epitaphs from the eighteenth or nineteenth century.

"Why doesn't anybody know what day it is? I want to know what day it is," Cassy whined.

Frankly, I was growing tired of her personality on drugs, and the way I was coming to know her then made me feel sort of aggressive. Or at least I was newly aware of an aggressive possibility in me under the influence of the whippet, and I didn't like this new knowledge about myself. I wanted to laugh, to experience the good feelings Derrick and Cassy had promised.

Derrick had been silent for a while and then suddenly spoke up with a clear pitch of curiosity. "Well, well, well, what do we have over there?"

"D-Rock?"

"Shhhh." He waved a hand at Cassy, who dropped her head and sulked.

"Sorry, babe."

Derrick was focused on something in the distance, something not too far off in the distance, though, since the night was a solid, unrelenting black. He took a gulp of the liquor store wine, right from the bottle we had been passing around between us, and then tipped his head back and guzzled every last bit.

Cassy grabbed at the air. "Hey! Save some for us!"

"You can have some beer," Derrick replied absently. Cassy reached for the bottle in a childish, pleading way, but Derrick sprang to his feet, bottle in hand, and started walking toward a dark figure making its way down a row of tombstones not too far from ours. The figure stopped walking and leaned forward, gradually becoming distinguishable. Derrick stopped walking, too, and watched the figure, which turned out to be a man on a late-night stroll with his pet dog. I heard the rustling sound of a plastic bag as the man removed it from his jacket pocket to collect, I presume, his dog's business.

"Good boy. Thatta boy. Want a treat, eh? Want a treat?" The man sounded like a perfectly ordinary man, the kind who likes animals more than people maybe, which was why he was on a late-night stroll with his dog instead of another person. The dog was almost impossible to see in the dark it was such a little thing, a smudge bigger than a lapdog, and suddenly the idea of such an ordinary man with such an ordinary dog was intolerably amusing to me. To Cassy also, for she giggled, quietly at first, and then more loudly when the man straightened himself up and called out, "Hello?"

The little dog yapped protectively.

"Hello," replied Derrick, friendly and animated. He resumed walking toward the man, and Cassy grabbed my arm. The tombstone I was sitting on moved out from under me, or maybe Cassy had pulled me onto hers with the fervor of her grip.

"My name's Derrick, what's yours?" Derrick was in front of the man, and the dog was yapping wildly. From where we sat I could only see Derrick's back and the outline of the dog as it bobbed up and down.

Cassy was reaching the peak of her high. I was, too. "It looks like a little gremlin," she declared, lacing her arms around my waist and burying her head in my jacket.

I heard Derrick say to the man, "Give me a high-five," and saw him raise an arm in the air like he always did with me, and so I assumed the man was somebody he knew and soon the two would be walking over to us, Derrick ready with an introduction. "Yeah, this is my friend so-and-so."

I didn't know what the howling was at first, didn't realize it was the man and not the dog making that God-awful, inhuman sound until I saw Derrick make a kicking motion and send the little bobbing creature hurtling through the air. It landed a few feet away from me and Cassy, that's how I knew the howling wasn't the dog, landed against an upright tombstone and had its little bones cracked like twigs. Thing is, it looked like a stuffed animal, not a real dog. There was no blood, and the animal's warm body looked stuffed to the stitches. Cassy was thrilled. She wanted to touch the dog, but I knew better from my experiences back in Montreal.

"Let it be," I said, feeling a sense of protectiveness over her. I took her hand and pulled us to our feet and led us over to Derrick. The awful howling had stopped and Derrick stood heaving, towering over the man's fetal body. His nostrils expanded and contracted rapidly, and his eyes were bright with excitement.

"Fucking guy! Fucking guy! Asked him for a high-five and he raises his hand to me! Fucking guy!" Derrick tapped the toe of his Kodiak against the man's side. "Get up! Get the fuck up and stop being such a fucking weak-ass!" The man whimpered and attempted to raise a hand to his head, but another, more assertive tap from Derrick seemed to exhaust him entirely. The man's arm fell to the ground; the man fell silent.

Cassy tripped into hysterics. "What happened? What happened?"

Derrick presented the forty-ounce, still unopened and perfectly intact, a thick film of blood on one side.

Cassy grabbed the bottle. "Holy shit it didn't break! It didn't break! It's like the bottle of stone!"

The three of us looked at the bottle and then at each other, at the man on the ground, and I said, "He's gonna have a shiner tomorrow," and then we left.

I honestly can't recall if we left the graveyard walking or running. Derrick and Cassy were ahead of me, invisible in the dark, but I could hear the quickening thuds of their boots on the ground, see the smoky labor of their breaths as they huffed and puffed to nowhere in particular. We ran and I thought of Avril, of Avril having been right to warn me that Derrick was trouble, and I knew I could count on her to be on my side. The thought of Avril on my side filled me with confidence and, finally, those feelings Derrick and Cassy had promised. The adrenaline was so intense I still remember how the ground felt. Like it was made of tiny springs and with each step we took we were bounced along like those little rubber balls you get from gumball machines. Derrick was bouncing, Cassy was bouncing and giggling, I was right behind. The tombstones looked like soft black wads of cotton randomly dotting the graveyard, and I wanted to touch each one. I wanted to feel everything around me, even Derrick and Cassy. But Derrick was too fascinated with the blood on his beer bottle and Cassy was too fascinated with her boyfriend and his bloody beer bottle. We were all too fascinated to comprehend what had happened moments before, and maybe if I hadn't been so high that night I could have, and probably I would have, stopped Derrick from beating that unlucky man as badly as he did. I knew that when my mother found out she would start to wail and tell me how it pained her that I had turned out simple-minded, that I would never amount to anything.

ISABELLE'S HAUNTING

"I wish I could have known Isabelle."

Madame Jasmin always chuckled one of her throaty smoker's chuckles when I said this, twining her arthritic claws through my hair and cautioning, "Be careful what you ask for, *ma princesse.*" I had such a sweet face, she said, and such perfect ringlets I would have put Shirley Temple out of business. My innocence was priceless.

Royle once told me Madame Jasmin brought men to my bedroom at night, allowing them to peek in as I slept on the bottom level of the bunk bed, unaware. The staircase leading from the main floor to the attic was at the south end of the house. My room was on the second floor, across from Madame Jasmin's at the north end. "So you don't hear the stairs creaking when she sneaks men up to your room," Royle claimed. His bedroom was in the attic.

Madame Jasmin scowled when I asked if this was true. Royle was too confident for his age, she said. Some kids thought they knew everything. "I don't want you in the attic because there's a draft. I need you in good health, *ma belle.*"

Royle liked to keep the attic window open, especially during winter, and sit on the ledge, dangling his spindly legs down the exterior wood paneling. He would sway there for hours at a time, imagining a tightrope extending from underneath his bare white feet to the peak of the mountain. His eyes would lock onto the ski-lift shuttling people to the top, lips forming muted words of encouragement as he braved his way across the only thing separating him from death. As long as Royle had a dream, I knew he was okay.

I wanted to be a painter, so I would sketch my brother as he dreamed, doing my best with scrap paper and crayons to make his vision real. Year after year, from the time Royle and I were placed in foster care at age eleven, Madame Jasmin promised me a set of paints for my birthday, but business always increased during the holiday season, and she would purchase a new Christmas outfit for me instead.

"Ask Monsieur Bergeron or Monsieur Dubois," Royle said one year. "They bring you all kinds of other gifts."

But those gifts, antique wooden toys with stiff limbs and chipped eyes, were really for Isabelle, and my slipping out of character would have been a violation of Madame Jasmin's Golden Rule.

Madame Jasmin had lived in the historic A-frame house with her husband, Monsieur Gallant, until he died from lung failure. Monsieur Gallant had never smoked a day in his life and would not tolerate his wife's habit indoors. It was only during his last days, when she had to be at his bedside every hour to clean the blood and phlegm that leaked freely down his chin, that he relented.

"I was so *nerveuse*," Madame Jasmin told us on one of her softer days. "I knew he was going to die, but you don't realize how long it feels to wait for that final moment until you are actually waiting."

When Monsieur Gallant finally took his last breath, she was ordering her next carton of cigarettes at the import boutique one mile away.

Madame Jasmin never had children, even though Monsieur Gallant had pleaded with her often to reconsider. He had been a handsome man, judging by the sepia photographs hanging above the fireplace in the living room, and Madame Jasmin had been striking in her youth. Her story changed a little each time she told it, but in truth she had met Monsieur Gallant at a silent auction. She went there that evening in search of Cubist paintings and returned home with the artist.

"It was *le coup de foudre*. There he was in his three-piece tailcoat suit, all pinstripes and smiles, and I knew he was the one."

Royle wagged his finger. "Last time you said he had a cane."

"*Oui*, he did," Madame Jasmin said, an ambiguous curve to her lips. "And he leaned against it like he was much older than he was. *Très charmant.*"

"But he was much older than you, right?"

"Yes, *petit gamin*. But at that time his cane was for his public image, not his health. You will understand this some day."

Le Pionnier, as the house was known, had a history of hauntings. Supposedly its first owners, a wealthy husband and wife with five children, purchased it custom-built in the fall of nineteen thirty-nine and died inexplicable deaths beginning one month later. First it was the youngest child, infant Valérie, who was found lying face down in her crib in October. The autopsy revealed she had drowned in lung fluid, but the cause was neither viral nor bacterial. The following month it was the twins, toddlers Benoît and Pierre Lamont. They awoke in the middle of the night convulsing, gasping for air as they called out to their parents, and by morning there were two more stiff bodies in the hospital morgue. Twelve-year-old Isabelle was the next to go, but her death was never confirmed. Her bed was found empty on the December after the twins' deaths, not a crease in the sheets or an imprint on the pillow, even though Madame Lamont swore on her dead children's graves she had tucked Isabelle in the night before. Isabelle had been a difficult child, however, suffering from bouts of what they called "hysteria" in those days, so her "death" was considered a blessing.

By January nineteen-forty the family was three: Monsieur Lamont, Madame Lamont, and their eldest child, Yvon. The town waited with held breath all month, as any day could mark the calendar with another Lamont death. January came and went and so did most of the new year, until one morning in November when the maid went to the attic for her broom and dustpan and found Monsieur and Madame Lamont and son Yvon on the floor, blood and phlegm stained down the sides of their shocked faces.

The house opened for sale a few weeks later, but nobody wanted to live there. People clomped through the empty giant in packs, posing as prospective buyers just to get an inside view of the castle of horrors; nobody made so much as a paltry offer on the place. In nineteen forty-one the town assumed responsibility for the house and turned it into a bed-and-breakfast for skiers. *Le Pionnier* could host up to twelve guests between its six bedrooms on the second floor, and the in-house staff shared quarters in the basement.

Isabelle's bedroom, which became mine once I was placed in the house, was the most popular; it had been preserved right down to her wardrobe of smocked nightgowns. The room was adorned floor to ceiling with brittle, curling sheets of Isabelle's couplets, inspired by the gloomy conceits of her favorite poet, Émile Nélligan. The walls underneath were a deep rose color, hairlines of wood showing through in places where Isabelle had scraped her nails during bouts of hysteria. Guests who stayed in the room were usually intrepid young adults on their first unsupervised outings, craving the thrill of sleeping on the "bunk bed of insanity".

Le Pionnier ran as a successful operation until November of nineteen-fifty, when two guests were found lifeless under the pink wool blankets of the bunk bed. Both girls were discovered on their backs, blood and phlegm crusted on their faces just like the final round of Lamont deaths on the same morning ten years earlier. But there was something more unsettling about the finding, which became known as "Isabelle's Haunting": the girl on the bottom bunk lay with one arm over the edge of the bed, wrist contorted so that the palm of her hand faced the floor. Her hand, as with the rest of her body, was bone rigid, and her fingers were pressed to the floor as though she had been pushing against it. Perhaps because the commotion of death occupied everybody's attention at first, nobody noticed until later the hairline scratches on the floor underneath where the girl's fingers had twitched with life for the last time.

Once again *Le Pionnier* opened for sale and people filed in to take a morbid look, but nobody proposed to stay after sunset. The house operated as a daytime ski lodge for a few seasons until business suffered when a new bed-and-breakfast opened at the top of the mountain. In nineteen fifty-three the house was vacated entirely; nobody even bothered to cover the furniture or board the windows and doors. A "No Trespassing" sign was posted in the front yard, and for seven years more the house remained vacant. The town ignored its growing decay, paid no attention to the midnight reverberations of beer bottles clanging against its sides. People joked that Isabelle had returned home whenever attention-seeking teenagers swore they had seen somebody rocking back and forth under the frame of the front door. It was a good joke, the town thought, for the front door of *Le Pionnier* had been replaced with a wound as wide as the wrecking ball that had finally begun to demolish the house.

That was when Madame Jasmin met her *coup de foudre*, in nineteen-sixty, and although she refused to bear children for him, she had no qualms about spending his money as though she had borne him many. Overnight *Le Pionnier* became the town tourist trap, the haunted house at the foot of the mountain. Madame Jasmin had researched its history thoroughly and employed her keen business sense to turn horror into income. In the beginning years, *Le Pionnier* was renowned for its haunted dinner theatres and promised apparition of twelve-year-old Isabelle Lamont. As there was no guarantee she would appear, a list of regular, curious guests began to build. Madame Jasmin kept guests entertained with acts like Yvon, the fourteen-year-old bellboy with fake blood and phlegm caked onto his face, and the mute Monsieur Lamont look-alike butler who hovered around the dinner table. If guests grew impatient, Madame Jasmin would retrieve one of infant Valérie's dolls from the attic, sit it in a splintered highchair at the head of the table, and babble to the doll as though it were Valérie and she were Madame Lamont. Nobody ever had the nerve to comment about Isabelle's non-apparitions after spectacles like that.

Monsieur Gallant, generous husband that he was, permitted his wife to do whatever she pleased with *Le Pionnier* as long as he could seek privacy in the attic, where he spent endless hours taking apart soft, beautiful things and reconstructing them into objects of appalling disfigurement. When I first arrived at the house in nineteen-seventy, five years after Monsieur Gallant's death, Madame Jasmin had to remove his paintings from the walls because the lopsided triangular eye of a man, or the hollow black square of mouth on a woman would lurch me into nightmarish sleep. The painting that both frightened and fascinated me the most was Monsieur Gallant's last, his vision of how Isabelle had looked the night she disappeared.

According to the photographs in the Lamont family album, Isabelle's hair had been abundantly blond and curly, and her expression apologetic, even when she smiled. A beautiful, solemn child. Yet, Monsieur Gallant hacked her apart and patched her back together with uneven red gaps for eyes and a diamond-shaped mouth cut into an unending scream. Her hair rotated around a boxy head in spokes of bright yellow, and her hands wrapped around her throat as though they were somebody else's hands trying to strangle her. Madame Jasmin insisted the painting remain in the hallway outside my bedroom door. Whenever I had the courage to look at it, I felt the impulse to scratch away at the paint, wondering if the canvas underneath would be bruised from the scream caught in Isabelle's throat.

Madame Jasmin kept *Le Pionnier* running after her husband's death—if anything, she was forced to in order to afford the land taxes. By nineteen sixty-five the little-known town had expanded to a population of five thousand; the baby boomers had moved in with the intention of transforming it into a thriving exurb. They tore through forest at the base of the mountain and paved the roads to gated communities and specialty shops. They opened cafés, restaurants, and schools. They even opened a racquet club, yet the economy idled. There weren't enough children to fill the schools, for the affluent townspeople worked in the city and were too tired at the end of their long commuter days to do anything but delay plans to procreate, or sit in a café and read, or dine out, or participate in a swift match of racquetball. And so, in nineteen sixty-nine, the mayor launched a campaign to invigorate the economy: Any family that produced offspring during the next five years would receive a check for one thousand, tax-free dollars for the first child, and five hundred dollars for every subsequent one, in addition to a one-hundred-dollar increase to the monthly family allowance of every child they already had.

By then Madame Jasmin was forty-five and widowed, so "producing" was out of the question. Acquiring, however, was not. Cecile, one of Le Pionnier's regulars, had been fostering children for years, and she informed Madame Jasmin that the town looked favorably upon this. Whatever it took to ensure growth and prosperity. As long as the kids were viewed as contributions toward the town's wellbeing. Madame Jasmin wasn't thrilled with the idea of bringing waifs into her home, but, as they say, money talks. If she could find a young adolescent boy who looked like Yvon Lamont, then she would no longer require a paid actor's service. There was no way she could enlist a child to play the role of Monsieur Lamont, but he wasn't absolutely necessary. A girl. She needed a girl who looked like Isabelle to revive the lost effect of Le Pionnier's haunted dinner theatres. That was when my life and Royle's became what I remember.

We had been wards of the government since birth; our parents left the hospital without us, and three months later we were placed in an orphanage. My memories of the years before Madame Jasmin are sparse and unreliable. Mostly I remember sounds, especially the thin, mournful voice of a choirgirl, which I surely dreamt up because life at the orphanage did not include trips to the choir. Royle refused to have memories, and his gift for imagining wonderful, impossible things made him cynical toward our reality and those who controlled it. Grown-ups were always amused by his relentless quests to expose inconsistencies in their words, and they never seemed concerned when he actually did. Royle was fascinated by the way grown-ups toed the line of truth like a game of hopscotch, and his fascination gradually developed into an obsession with tightrope walking.

Madame Jasmin wanted only me at first. She swished into the city orphanage, x-rayed the children's playroom from behind ornate fuscia-rimmed glasses, and then pointed to Royle, who sat listlessly in a corner.

"Him. I want a girl just like him."

The House Mother grinned like she had just won the lottery. She had been trying to get rid of us for years—by then we were the oldest kids in the orphanage—but as soon as prospective parents learned we came as a pair, they shifted their eyes to a scrawny ringbone kid drowning in a handed-down nightshirt and said, "That one's cute. Don't you think, dear?"

Madame Jasmin smacked her hands together when the House Mother pulled me out from behind the bookshelf, and she jammed a crooked finger through one of my ringlets when she learned I had never taken ill a day in my life. "*Bonne petite gamine!*"

Royle glared from his corner, squeezing himself between his arms and humming the theme song from Alfred's Hitchcock's *Psycho*.

The House Mother eyed me warningly.

I knew the routine: Royle and I were to wait in the playroom while she served Madame Jasmin hot cocoa and assured her that it might seem a bit much at first, two kids, but in fact we were unusually gifted and destined for great things. That was why we were the oldest ones at the orphanage: We were too special to send home with just anybody.

"She's crazy," Royle chanted between breaths of *Psycho*.

"We're not going anywhere."

"You mean I'm not going anywhere. And by the time I find you, you'll be married to some French guy with stupid glasses." Royle's mouth bunched into a little rosebud, his face ascetic as he focused on an invisible tightrope. I watched the adrenaline dilate his pupils, the rush of height color his cheeks, and then reached for my pencil and paper and began to sketch. We routinely lost hours doing this, living in our own world, so who knows how long the House Mother had needed to secure her victory.

"Monsieur Gallant was a painter," Madame Jasmin said, leaning over me. Her nostrils flared with irritation when she said hello to Royle and was received by a grunt. She turned her back to him and stepped between us, and right then I knew I had to put my brother first.

"We'll run away," I told the House Mother, who loomed behind Madame Jasmin.

"Don't be so childish. Madame Jasmin owns a very famous haunted house. You'll be the best-dressed kids every year on Halloween."

I returned to my sketch, and Royle resumed his rendition of *Psycho*.

The House Mother spoke into Madame Jasmin's ear. "The boy's a bit shy. You'll want to keep them in the same bedroom at first."

"Of course."

"You may pass by next week to collect the check. In the meantime, I'm sure the bonuses will be sufficient to start you off."

The conversation continued as the old and new mothers left the playroom, but Royle had heard enough to know. "That crazy woman is being paid to take me. She wants you, but the orphanage had to *sell* me to her."

All I could do was take my brother's hand and lead him to our bedroom, where he sat on his plastic-covered cot and sulked while I divided our modest possessions among kids in the orphanage who had none.

Madame Jasmin put Royle to work immediately; just minutes after welcoming us to *Le Pionnier* and telling rather than showing us where everything was, she held a framed, water-stained photograph of Yvon Lamont next to his head. "You see, *petit gamin*, you have the same hair color."

"That's because the picture's old and yellow. And you said Yvon was fourteen. I'm eleven."

Though it was apparent she disliked Royle in the way she pressed her fingertips to her temples, Madame Jasmin kept her sentiments from thwarting her business sense. A witty ghost for a bellboy, what a treat for dinner guests! Of course Royle was cynical, not witty, but guests who attended the dinner theatres were too much in awe to know the difference.

We were homeschooled on weekdays by Cecile, the *Pionnier* regular who had enticed Madame Jasmin into becoming a foster parent. Cecile arrived every day at nine o'clock sharp with two of her wards, Marc and Manon, and spent mornings teaching us grammar and arithmetic. Marc was fourteen and Manon nine, and the two reminded me of mice the way they tiptoed into the parlor at the back of the house and wrinkled their noses at its musty smell. Madame Jasmin had restored the parlor to look like it had in nineteen thirty-nine. The Lamont children had been homeschooled, and she was determined to recreate the environment in which they had learned, even insisting Cecile use the ruler if we disobeyed. Royle disobeyed often, but never when Cecile was near. Though Marc and Manon would eye him warningly, they never tattled because his odd behaviors made them nervous.

"There's something wrong with your brother," Manon told me one recess, as Royle treaded across the parlor with arms extended at his sides like an airplane, each bare white foot stepping precisely in front of the other.

"No, there isn't," I said, suppressing my urge to twist her nose like a bottle cap. "He can talk to the dead. He's met the Lamonts."

Royle must have heard me for he started muttering to himself as he traveled the room, rolling his eyes back until only the whites showed.

"See? He's talking to Isabelle right now."

We spent afternoons doing arts and crafts, as Cecile informed Madame Jasmin that all quality schools included these in their *curricula*. Marc and Manon got to do whatever they pleased, usually maladroit scribbling or half-wit attempts at building popsicle-stick houses, while Cecile made Royle paint.

"Your sister's an artist," she tried, when at first he merely skated his eyes over her poor excuse for a paint set—an old newspaper, a split-haired brush, and a can of oily industrial paint.

Royle didn't approve of being insulted; however, I could feel Madame Jasmin watching us from the hallway, so I spread a piece of newspaper across Royle's tablet desk and stuck the paintbrush in his hand.

"Paint me while I walk the tightrope."

"You don't walk the tightrope."

"Then I'll sing and you paint the story I'm telling."

"Dance, too," Royle said, dipping his brush into the paint and swirling it around lackadaisically. "Sing that song the choirgirl sings, and dance like Isabelle Lamont would have danced."

Madame Jasmin leaned against the parlor doorframe, perked with interest. Despite my cottonmouth, I went to the center of the room and pointed then flexed each foot as I begged my memories for the lyrics to the choirgirl's song. After a minute of suffocating inability, I began to sing, humming at first as my legs worked independently from the rest of my body and swept me around the room. I closed my eyes as the sounds coming from my throat began to form into words, and I imagined I was the paintbrush in Royle's hand, skimming across the paper from the safety of warm, familiar fingers. I had never sung the choirgirl's song before; it had been only a vague memory until then. And yet, my diaphragm lifted the lyrics to my consciousness, my limbs retrieved memories from Isabelle's short life at Le Pionnier, and I danced before eyes that were perfectly blind to what was really happening. From that moment on, Madame Jasmin took complete charge of my life.

First she withdrew me from homeschooling and enrolled me in a finishing course for girls. She drove me to class each morning and trusted other mothers to return me safely while she attended to dinner guests. One week into my new formative education, Madame Jasmin terminated Cecile's services and took charge of Royle's homeschooling. Like before, he spent mornings learning grammar and arithmetic, but afternoons under Madame Jasmin's tutelage were without plan or structure. She scolded him for spending his free time staring out the attic window, but she never encouraged him to do otherwise. If anything, she enabled his lassitude; with little else to interest or distract him, Royle would reliably appear in his smart bellboy suit every day at five o'clock, sour-faced from boredom and ready to cater to dinner guests.

After I completed the finishing course, Madame Jasmin enrolled me in ballet. Then piano, then voice, and then a specialized history course about how girls thought, behaved, and dressed in the nineteen-thirties. This went on until Royle and I turned twelve, by which time I could converse demurely about the Great Depression, hum every Glenn Miller and Django Reinhardt tune, and angle a cloche hat on my head just right.

"You're different now," Royle said on the evening of our twelfth birthday. We were sitting at the dinner table waiting for Madame Jasmin to light the candles on our cake.

"I'm more mature now."

"Madame Jasmin says I can start public school soon."

"I'm going to private school."

"I think she has different plans for you."

"Happy birthday to you! Happy birthday to you! Happy birthday, *chers gamins*, happy birthday to you!" Madame Jasmin entered the dining room grinning behind a mountain of chocolate, Royle's favorite, topped with twelve hissing sparklers—one of the few thoughtful gestures she ever extended to him. The layered cake glistened with icing and our names looped across the top in raspberry jelly. Royle looked away when Madame Jasmin presented the knife so he could make the first cut. Used to his antics by then, she handed the knife to me.

"Well! *Le Pionnier's* dinner theatre days are over. No more Yvon Lamont for you, Royle. You can start public school now."

I felt like she was speaking to me through Royle, who pursed his mouth as if to say, "Told you."

"And you, *ma belle* Fancy, are ready to begin your work."

"My work?"

"Yes, *princesse*, nothing in life is free. Your brother has learned this, and now it's your turn."

"I don't understand."

"I will need somebody to keep our guests company when they come to spend time in the house."

"It's going to be a ski lodge again?"

"No, *gamine*, a place for people who are curious about its history, like a museum."

"Oh." But we didn't have any artifacts except for Isabelle's bedroom set, which had become mine, and which I wasn't willing to share with strangers. There were also Monsieur Gallant's paintings stored in the attic, and I wasn't eager to see them splayed along *Le Pionnier's* walls again.

Madame Jasmin rubbed her hands together and smiled. "This house has so much unsolved history. So many things have happened here with no explanation. *La mort*, for example; there has been a lot of that but nobody knows why. Some people are fascinated by this and willing to pay to just be here, to feel the energies."

And other people, men, were willing to pay large sums of money to meet the legendary Isabelle Lamont.

"I can't believe you don't think she's crazy," Royle said later, when we were alone in the attic.

I swiveled my head side to side and studied my features in the pink and gold hand mirror Madame Jasmin had given me after dinner. "I could be the perfect Isabelle, don't you think? I kind of look like her."

"Isabelle was just a girl. I bet you she died like the rest of the Lamont family, from some lung disease. The town just wanted to be famous so it made up a story."

"Then what about those two girls who died in her room ten years later?"

"People die all the time, Fancy. This house is so old people are going to die in it."

Sweet Royle could be too confident sometimes. This infuriated Madam Jasmin, but she never truly understood my brother. She treated his mood swings between listlessness and insolence like different personalities, and occasionally she threatened to return him to the orphanage if he didn't pick one, preferably the former, and stick with it.

"I just think it would be fun, Royle. You got to be Yvon for a year."

"She made me."

"Just be happy we're together, okay?"

Royle slipped down from the window ledge and ducked under his cot, reappearing with a box of scrap paper and mottled crayons. "Now that you aren't taking all those girl classes you can draw again."

Drawing. I had forgotten all about it during that last year.

Every paper in the box was crowded with images. I couldn't discern what the images were supposed to be, but I knew their sharp lines and angles came from Royle's meticulous hand.

"Are these from Cecile's classes?"

"I never did anything for her again after you left."

"When did you do these?"

"When you were gone to your girl classes."

My chest hurt as I studied Royle's drawings; some of the indents on the pages were so deep the paper had torn. I could tell he had been determined to create something I would like, something soft and flowing and not brutal like Monsieur Gallant's Cubist paintings, the only artwork he had ever been exposed to. My brother, in silent, defiant response to my absence during that last year, had used drawing as a way to keep me close. This was clear in the desperate, repeating patterns of his work.

"When I'm better I'll make something for the hallway so you won't have nightmares anymore."

Royle looked so vulnerable standing in front of me with his offering, a small boy seeking his mother's approval. I couldn't bring myself to tell him I hadn't had a nightmare in a while, though I couldn't remember when they had ceased, or why.

The following morning Madame Jasmin took me to the tailor's, along with Isabelle's preserved wardrobe. Monsieur Bergeron knew all about the Lamonts, for his father had run the shop when the family purchased *Le Pionnier* in nineteen thirty-nine. He scanned me from head to toe with wide-set bulging eyes and nodded like a satisfied army general when Madame Jasmin announced I would be impersonating Isabelle.

"I hope you won't disobey too much, *ma chouette*," he said, snaking his measuring tape under my arms and around my chest.

I blushed and told him no, I would just look like Isabelle and maybe talk to some of *Le Pionnier's* visitors about her. Monsieur Bergeron seemed disappointed with my reply, so I looked to Madame Jasmin for instruction.

"Fancy...Isabelle will entertain guests as they wish. I already have a list of people waiting to meet her. Perhaps, since you always give me such generous discounts, I could add you?"

After we left, she informed me that from then on, whenever we had guests or she brought me somewhere in relation to my role as Isabelle Lamont, I was to introduce myself as Isabelle.

The new business started gradually, guests visiting *Le Pionnier* on weekdays for afternoon coffee and pastries with Madame Jasmin. They sat in the living room and discussed *les jours du passé*, oohing and ahhing as they pored through the Lamont family album. The week before Madame Jasmin opened the house to guests, she commissioned an antique reproductions company to transform the living room (except the windows, which were sealed up) into the one from the Lamont album. Wall sconces with pleated gold silk shades were mounted at even intervals around the room. A rust-brown fringe chandelier was installed above the curved-back Eloise sofa, where guests could sit and enjoy the glow of the fireplace while they perused the photo album. Burled walnut smoking stands bookended both sides of the sofa, and a card table across from the sofa boasted a genuine Victor Victrola, Guy Lombardo's "Enjoy Yourself" spinning softly under the needle. Madame Jasmin chose floral-print wallpaper reminiscent of a springtime meadow to create the illusion of light and space, and her finishing touch was the tufted gold chenille Cleopatra bench beside the Victrola, where I was to sit whenever guests asked to meet Isabelle Lamont.

My services weren't required at first, even though Madame Jasmin made me dress up and wait in the parlor while she sat with guests. Monsieur Bergeron had adjusted Isabelle's wardrobe to fit me properly, but I didn't feel comfortable in the maize rayon skirts or taffeta plaid gloves. My head hurt from wearing my hair in tight braids, and my thick, curled bangs made me look like a Nancy Ann Storybook Doll. Although young girls weren't supposed to wear make-up in the nineteen-thirties, Madame Jasmin patted rouge on my cheeks and gloss on my lips to make them look fuller.

"You look like a clown," Royle said one afternoon, as I sat at his old school desk, carving *IL* into the wood.

I arched my back to escape the scratch of my blouse. "I do not."

"Have you been sitting here all afternoon?" Royle glanced over his shoulder before entering the parlor. Madame Jasmin had told him that as long as I was working, he was to either join some after-school activity or use the back entrance to the house and wait in the basement until the last guest left.

I rose to offer Royle his desk, but instead he took my hand and led me to the doorframe. "Listen."

I leaned into the hallway and listened.

"She sleeps *comme un bébé*, Monsieur Dubois. I promise you."

"So she heard nothing last night?"

"*Rien.* Would you like to schedule another viewing? Friday nights are quite popular. She's had such a long week by then."

I looked at Royle. "What are they talking about?"

"You. I wasn't lying."

I had never accused Royle of lying, but just the thought alone of men watching me sleep seemed ridiculous. Why would they do that? I heard Monsieur Dubois click his tongue as Madame Jasmin described what I was wearing at that moment and would he like to have a sitting with me?

Royle let go of my hand and kicked his bare foot against the doorframe. "You're like her show-and-tell."

I made a shushing motion and tried to follow the rest of Madame Jasmin's conversation with Monsieur Dubois, but the topic moved from me to town gossip. When I turned my attention to Royle, he crossed his arms over his chest. "I want to be with you when you meet that man."

Sweet Royle. His jealousy was so sincere I actually considered his demand, but in the end I could not disobey the house rules and let him suffer the consequences.

Later, after Madame Jasmin was locked in her bedroom crying herself to sleep with a romance novel, I went to the attic and sat with Royle. "Hey, baby brother."

Even though we were twins, I had always felt older, more able to accept what our lives were and move from day to day without letting my frustrations control me. Royle was the more sensitive one, more fragile, which was why he needed me to watch over him.

"How was the sitting with that man?"

"Monsieur Dubois was very polite. He gave me a handcrafted miniature rocking horse for my night table. He said I used to have one I could ride, but I'm too old for that now."

"Isabelle."

"What?"

"Isabelle used to have a rocking horse she could ride. We never had toys."

I tousled Royle's hair and laughed. "Isabelle. Yes, Isabelle had a rocking horse."

Monsieur Dubois must have told his friends about me, for suddenly I had daily sittings with different men. Sitting hours were from one to five Monday through Friday, after my homeschooling with Madame Jasmin. I was free to do as I pleased evenings and weekends, as was Royle, and I was disappointed that my brother chose to isolate himself.

"Haven't you made any friends at school?" I asked, shortly after our thirteenth birthday.

Madame Jasmin had once again promised me a paint set and ordered a tailored low-hemmed ankle skirt from Monsieur Bergeron instead, but much to my surprise she gave Royle a sketchpad and some charcoal. Despite her disdain for him by that point, she was evidently pleased that his artwork was beginning to resemble her late husband's.

"Why don't you invite a friend over this weekend?"

"I saw a guy outside your room again last night."

"What guy? How?"

"I just did."

"You were spying on me?"

I felt as though Royle had been trying to punish me lately. He had started ignoring me at the dinner table and any other time Madame Jasmin was around, so the only place I could access him was in the attic. Even there he barely acknowledged me. One time, he drew a thick charcoal line down the center of the attic and walked across it in his bare feet, and then stomped black prints through the house until Madame Jasmin hurled the mop and bucket at him and split open his bottom lip.

"What do you talk about with those men, Fancy?" Royle's hair was stuck to his face in greasy strips, and his body gave off an odor that reminded me of the orphanage. "Do they make you call them *father*?"

"Stop it."

"Then tell those men to stop calling you Isabelle."

But how could I? I had grown to love the girl who had disappeared from *Le Pionnier* in the winter of nineteen thirty-nine; I loved her like a sister. I had memorized every poem she had written and discovered why she had felt a connection to the words of Émile Nélligan. I had even begun to decipher what she had scratched onto the rose-colored walls of her bedroom. "I think she was asking for help."

Royle pulled at his bed sheet to turn it down. "I'm tired now."

"Oh. Well, goodnight." I rose to leave and found myself looking straight into the eyes of Monsieur Gallant's Isabelle, sitting on top of a chest of drawers Royle had dragged out of storage. Isabelle screamed her silent, unending scream, and my ears started to ring. "What is this doing here?"

Royle rushed over and stood between the painting and me, though I couldn't tell which he was trying to protect. "You hate it, so what's the difference?"

"Madame Jasmin will kill you if she finds out!"

"It's been here for months."

That night I was determined to prove my brother wrong…and yet, I also felt exhilarated by the possibility he was right. Men were willing to see me even in sleep? What did they think about as they watched me? Did they find me pretty? In order to stay awake in the dark, I recited Émile Nélligan's "*La fuite de l'enfance*" in my head. Over and over again, I recited the poem in ways I imagined Isabelle might have, fending off my growing fogginess until I heard a creak in the hallway floorboards.

Each footstep was slight and precise and sounded like it belonged to one person only. Was it Madame Jasmin coming to check on me? Had Royle been repeatedly fooled by the dark? I held my breath to take in as much sound as possible. The person was not wearing shoes, which would have been unusual for a guest; men who visited *Le Pionnier* never removed their shoes. I turned onto my side and faced the wall where the man's shadow would become visible against the hallway light that spilled into my room. I would watch his silhouette as he watched me, unaware.

I waited and waited but no silhouette appeared. The footsteps stopped, and I heard something brush against the wall outside my bedroom. Otherwise, the hallway was still. Then it occurred to me: Isabelle. Maybe Isabelle had returned home! Maybe she *had* disappeared in nineteen thirty-nine and not died like the town declared, and she had been trying to return home ever since. And so that was whom Royle had seen at my bedroom door, only he hadn't realized because it was dark and who would have expected Isabelle to return home after so many years? I rolled onto my back and exhaled giddily. "Isabelle?"

I heard a gasp, and my skin began to tingle. "It's okay," I said, sitting up and touching one foot at a time to the ground so as not to scare my visitor away. "Your room is just the way you left it. I always put everything back exactly where it was." Isabelle whimpered, and my body warmed; she was frightened, and I would make her feel safe. I opened the door and looked into the hallway, making sure my every movement was as beckoning and as gentle as possible.

Royle hunched forward and wrapped his arms around his bare torso. His body jerked back and forth as though he was having a seizure standing up, the tears dripping off his chin so thick they appeared opaque. "I heard noises in the hallway again."

I had opened my bedroom door to a worse horror than Monsieur Gallant's mutation of Isabelle—worse, even, than if the mutated Isabelle had come to life and stepped out of the painting. "You've been watching me, haven't you?"

Royle sniveled incomprehensibly and tried to squeeze past me into my bedroom. I blocked his entrance. "Haven't you?"

Before he could answer, Madame Jasmin's shadow expanded into the hallway like a hot-air balloon. "What's going on out here?"

I knew she would punish my brother severely if I told the truth.

"Royle had a nightmare."

Madame Jasmin screwed her eyes onto Royle, and for the first time I saw what she saw. Still, I had to behave like Isabelle would have if one of her younger siblings had awoken crying from a nightmare.

"Come on." I pointed at the staircase, and Royle stuck out his hand. I felt sick to my stomach, but I hooked my fingers through his and led him back to the attic, leaving Madame Jasmin to gawk at his exposed backside.

We never spoke about that night, but it was impossible to go back to the way things had been. Royle retreated further into himself, and Madame Jasmin lost all tolerance for him. When he refused to eat his meals, she threw them out and told him to starve. When he tracked charcoal through the house, she coolly handed me the mop. When he stayed out past dark, she locked all the doors, forcing Royle to scale the house and climb in through the attic window. And when he caught pneumonia the autumn before our fourteenth birthday, she waited until he was delirious from fever before phoning the doctor.

"I'll take you shopping for a paint set this weekend," Madame Jasmin said the night before our birthday.

"No, thank you. But maybe Royle would like one."

Royle looked up from his untouched dinner plate—not in anticipation of a new paint set, but in case I had finally forgiven him. I was surprised at how long I had held a grudge against him; my increasing popularity with *Le Pionnier's* patrons had obscured time, I guess. A year had changed my brother significantly. He was no longer shorter than I was, but four inches taller. And though he was thin from continual bouts of illness, his arms were remarkably muscular and his shoulders filled out the top of his T-shirt.

"I have something for you," he said. "For Isabelle, I mean. It's at school. I'll bring it home tomorrow." Royle pushed his chair back and retired to the attic.

Madame Jasmin patted my hand and whispered, "I hate to tell you, *gamine*, but there's something wrong with your brother."

Those familiar words didn't upset me like they once had.

I had to work the following day, even though it was my birthday.

"Tomorrow," Madame Jasmin promised. "Tomorrow you can take the day off."

But I didn't mind working; it had become my life, and I secretly dreaded weekends because I no longer had Royle to keep me company.

Monsieur Dubois brought me a leather-bound copy of Émile Nélligan's *Motifs Poétiques*, and Monsieur Castonguay, a new patron, presented me with Billie Holliday's *God Bless the Child* record.

"I hope you like your gift, *Isabelle*. Fourteen, *hein*? You are no longer a little girl!"

I bowed my head and smiled, the tickle from Monsieur Castonguay's attention spreading underneath the new maroon empire-waist dress Madame had given me that morning. "*Merci*, Monsieur Castonguay."

"Please, *ma belle Isabelle*, call me Father."

"*Oui, Papa.*"

Monsieur Castonguay leaned back on the Eloise sofa and spread his arms across the top. "Dance for me," he pleaded through trembling mouth. "Dance to Billie Holiday."

I rose from my Cleopatra bench and straightened my dress, but then a loud thud from the front entrance of *Le Pionnier* interrupted our sitting. Monsieur Castonguay snapped to his feet, and Madame Jasmin's heels click-clicked down the hallway. It was too late: Royle ran past her and into the sitting room, a large, gift-wrapped canvas secured under one arm.

"Fancy, you have to come with me."

Monsieur Castonguay looked from me to Royle, whom he knew absolutely nothing about, his mouth opening and closing as he fumbled to button his shirt.

Madame Jasmin caught up to Royle and slapped him across the face. He ducked and flinched as she flapped her arms and screamed at him, but he did not retreat.

"Come with me, Fancy, please."

Monsieur Castonguay deposited a humid kiss on my cheek and excused himself. "Sweet dreams, *Isabelle*."

Just like that, Madame Jasmin composed herself and ushered him out of the sitting room, one hand on his back as she confessed that she had brought home a new foster child, but things were not working out so the boy would be returned.

Royal dropped his canvas on the floor. "What's happened to you, Fancy?"

"You are not supposed to come in here while I am working."

My reply launched him into a frenzy. "Fancy, *please* listen to me! A guy at school–"

"What guy?"

"A friend! A friend, Fancy. You told me to make friends so I did!"

The front door slammed shut and I heard Madame Jasmin shriek and pound her hands on the wall. God knew how she would punish Royle. As he, too, sensed the inevitable, he started talking quickly, urgently. I could barely make sense of his words.

"...not normal...he told me he saw a movie about...Fancy, you don't have to—"

"My name is *Isabelle*."

Madame Jasmin was at Royle's side instantly, digging her claws into his neck and hauling him up the stairs; I had never seen her so nimble. The two fought brutally. They reached the second floor, and I heard visceral howls intercut with gurgling sounds. They reached the attic, and I heard fingertips scraping along the walls and objects crashing to the floor. A part of me wanted to beg Madame Jasmin to stop—lock me in the attic instead!—and through that impulse came my first real understanding of the word "hysteria". Maybe Isabelle Lamont had died from hysteria after all, run off in a fit like the one Royle was having and died, finally, unable to care for herself. No one would ever know, which struck me as a greater loss than Isabelle herself.

Madame Jasmin must have grown exhausted from struggling with Royle, for she didn't return to the sitting room after all the yelling and banging upstairs died down. An hour passed while I sat on my Cleopatra bench listening to Billie Holiday, hands folded neatly on my lap. It was dark outside when my stomach began to rumble for my birthday dinner. Would there still be a celebration tonight? I went to Royle's canvas and leaned it upright against the wall. The wrapping paper was inscribed, "For my sister on our fourteenth birthday." I unwrapped my gift slowly, enjoying the sound of its tear harmonizing with the gentle scratch of the Victrola. Royle had made me a real painting, not one of his angry charcoal sketches that stained everything it touched, and I wanted the feeling to last—the feeling of exhaling right before everything goes black, or breathing for the first time ever. I smiled as I gazed into the uneven red gaps that were my eyes. My hair rotated around a boxy head in spokes of bright yellow, and I warmed; Royle had always struggled with my ringlets. He had painted my hands differently than Monsieur Gallant had, not wrapped around my neck, and I realized that was what had terrified me about Monsieur Gallant's painting: Imagining I would ever want to hurt myself. But I didn't want to think about unpleasant things—it was my birthday—so I carried my gift upstairs and hung it on the wall outside my bedroom, and then I went to sleep with forgiveness in my heart. Sweet Royle had known after all.

BANANAS AND LIMES

After the last Saint James Lacop congregant passed away, the State repurposed the church as a meeting place for members of AA and other damned populations, but no one is damned enough to travel one hour northwest of Palmyra to a dirt cul-de-sac of six boarded-up farmhouses whose front porches are sunken and splintered open in places where people once rocked on chairs and smoked corncob pipes; the church's disrepair is a statement about how little 21st-century God participates in the lives of the dysfunctional and insolvent. Saint James once contained 20 hand-carved pews, an ornate pine lectern, and a gold-tasseled Persian rug, above which Christ, joyous in spite of the nails and thorns pillaging his flesh, smiled onto the priest during his late hours of worship and self-flagellation. It once boasted a blocky white cross on its roof; now, a wire forced into the approximate shape of an angel serves as a beacon for the lost.

Today, the lost are 47 children. All on their own, they've arranged themselves from youngest to oldest, smallest to biggest: infants and toddlers at the front, harnessed to a carousel of mechanical arms designed to rock them to sleep; a row of schoolchildren, both sexes; two rows of pre-pubescent boys; and a row of teenage girls against the wall at the very back. Like organ pipes, the girls lift up and down on their toes to keep sight of their young. Except when a mother visibly suppresses the instinct to tend to her fussing baby, no one from the group has retaliated, even mildly, against confinement to the church basement since eight o'clock this morning. An upbringing governed by the threat of eternal damnation has ensured tenacious obedience from these children, although they are not obeying anyone now in their stillness. Refusal to engage is the only way they know how to behave toward Outsiders. Any child who might know other possibilities—from sources prohibited within compound boundaries—must keep quiet in case He's listening through the mouthpieces clipped to the Outsiders' belts.

The group is of one oily complexion, which becomes overwhelmed by acne with age. The schoolchildren wear John Lennon-style glasses with thick dirty lenses that make their eyes appear to bulge as if from thyroid disease. The boys are gaunt, the girls are stout, and all of them, even the infants and toddlers, are dressed in white baptismal garments. As is often the nature of classified operations, someone from the compound learned of the impending raid, and at dawn this morning the community was ready. The mothers had just finished preparing the Flock when the convoy of Child Protective Services transport vans arrived. CPS encouraged the mothers to accompany their children to Saint James church, a discrete location where the children would be separated from one another and sent to transitional homes, but the mothers stood back, linked arm-in-arm in a neat crescent as their children were taken from them. This was a journey for the young alone, a lesson about the evils of the world. And so the children, noiseless, lifting the skirts of their garments in fists to avoid rain puddles, were herded into one set of vans, and the Fathers, smelling of tobacco and other pre-dawn immoralities, filed into the other.

"Do not allow the Outsiders to remove your garments!" the Fathers heralded. "Your garments are all that will protect you!"

It is noon. The children's excruciating docility has spread anxiety among the CPS team and church volunteers, who pace and crack their knuckles in wait for something to happen. No one anticipated a delay between the children being moved from one location to the next, but the unmarked black vehicle parked across from the church, likely media, has forced CPS into a waiting game.

Laird Fullerton, the intelligence behind Project Fumarase, can't look at the group any longer; what has driven him for the last two years now makes him want to puke. The faces all watch him in the same unblinking, iron-deficient way. Do their eyes *have* any color? The closest he can guess is gray, except even gray has something to it, a highlight of blue, green, or gold. Laird has seen what a child looks like after being locked in a cupboard for 18 months. He has watched nanny-cam footage of a seven-year-old solemnly dissecting a toy poodle. Once, undercover, he was solicited by a mother looking to rent out her little girl for a bump of meth. He has never seen children without basic features that make them unique.

Peggy Galvin, the newest addition to Project-F, walks the length of the group with a tray of juice boxes and crackers. She has offered snacks to the children regularly since their arrival. "You guys must at least be thirsty by now!"

The schoolchildren eye the snacks more desirously than their seniors, but their fingers, curving and curling, remain at their sides.

Peggy must win the group's trust by the end of the day, otherwise Laird will transfer her back to the windowless office filled with reports of missing persons whose loved ones have moved on. He was frank about why he invited her onboard: "We need someone with a soft touch." She would have liked to hear something more. Perhaps, "You're the right person for the job, Galvin. No matter what." She is the only woman on the team.

A girl speaks from the back row. "Ma'am? I need to feed my son."

When Peggy starts toward her with the tray, the girl huffs and points at her breasts. "I need to *feed* my son."

Her son could be any baby on the carousel; they're all genderless in their matching white garments. They've been supplied with a steady stream of formula since they arrived, and the church volunteers have been timely and efficient about diaper changing and burping. Except for one baby, who has rejected the bottle every time and writhes whenever anyone touches him. A fusty odor hangs in the air around him like wasps in the last days of summer.

"Bring a fresh bottle, please," Peggy tells a volunteer.

Mother's and son's matching flat noses are lost in the fleshiness of their faces, and their earlobes remind Peggy of scrotums. There's an absence of curiosity and intelligence about the young mother, but also an absence of the wrath stewing in the other children's expressions. Maybe this one will talk.

Project Fumarase, as the public understands it, is about rescuing children and prosecuting criminals. Few people know about its sinister purpose: to collect certain evidences before the State-issued warrant expires in three days and the children and Fathers have to be released. After that, the group will relocate like it did in 2005 and 2008. The men will continue to espouse their 12-year-old half-sisters and nieces, the recessive gene will continue to proliferate, babies will continue to be stillborn or severely deformed. Eventually the group will breed itself out of existence, but that could take another century.

"What do you mean, 'certain evidences'?" Peggy asked Laird when he first spoke to her about the project.

"Blood tests. We're looking for a specific enzyme."

"I mean the sexual abuse. How will you prove it if the kids won't talk?"

"They won't talk, Peggy. We know that already."

"I don't understand."

"We need the State to think it's about child sexual abuse or else we won't get funding. What we're really after is evidence of fumarase deficiency. Once we prove it's in these kids, we'll be able to do a lot more than arrest a few zealots and pedophiles. It'll be big, Galvin. Big."

"Who else breastfeeds?" Peggy asks the back row. Only the one girl breaks rank; the others close in on her empty space, eyes training after her with disapproval and envy.

"I want privacy," she says, puffing her torso against the scorn from the back row. Her right shoulder sags, like a dislocation never corrected.

"You can use the bathroom. I'll have to accompany you, but I'd like your consent."

"I don't consent."

"Charlie!" Peggy calls to the volunteers idling by the exit door. A scoliated man with pattern baldness steps forward. "Would you accompany this young lady to the bathroom?"

The girl looks at Charlie and scowls. "You said you needed my consent. You lied."

"I said I'd *like* it, and I thought you would appreciate the opportunity. It's up to you. If you're old enough to be a mother, you're old enough to make lesser choices."

Charlie, the other volunteers, even Laird, stare at Peggy like she's announced that a bomb is strapped to her chest and everyone's going to die. Her pulse speeds, pruritus spreads under her clothes. Why did Laird insist she come dressed for a business meeting? These children won't identity with her simply because she's female! In her black wool power-suit, she must look like Satan compared with the image surely looming in their minds right now: soft, safe mothers in pastel blue and eggshell pink floor-length dresses buttoned to the chin. Fathers in jeans and plaid shirts. Everyone, on days like today, in white.

Peggy's confidence wavers for the first time since Laird recruited her; she must prove her competency. She clicks her tongue at the girl like a disappointed older sister. The girl considers her, opens herself just enough to disclose that beyond the bovine dish of her face is a person who understands compromise. Perhaps she will be what CPS needs to destroy this community of outliers. Certainly, the destruction has already begun with the separation of the children from their mothers, the women from their husbands, and everyone from the Prophet, who was informed, like the rest of the community, about what was to come, but who did not, like the rest of the community, draw from the strength of faith and heavenly love. He's probably in Canada by now.

Peggy dismisses Charlie and unhooks the infant from the carousel. Above his congested protests, she asks once more if anyone else breast-feeds. The back row responds with furious silence. She passes the baby to his mother, and it's as though the group suddenly realizes what's happening—everything before now belonged to a reality that couldn't touch them under their white garments. It starts when a schoolgirl whispers, "Your son is going to Hell." A few more join her, and it graduates to a controlled chant. "Your son is going to Hell. Your son is going to Hell." In the short time it takes Peggy to lead the girl away, it escalates to a unanimous cry, with Laird and the volunteers watching in awe as the children point their index fingers toward the bathroom. "YOUR SON IS GOING TO HELL. YOUR SON IS GOING TO HELL."

The bathroom is miniscule and as malodorous as an outhouse. There's a plastic hand-mirror duct-taped to the wall above the sink. A sticky note on top of the toilet seat reads *lift flapper to flush*. Water from exposed, mold-covered pipes overhead drips into a tin wastebasket. Peggy empties the wastebasket into the toilet and lifts the flapper; the toilet belches and spits until all that remains is a tampon applicator floating in slow circles.

The girl clutches her baby to her chest and stares at the plastic mirror. Peggy wonders which is more devastating to her, being locked up with an Outsider, or seeing herself, probably for the first time in her life, removed from her reality. She flips the wastebasket over and sits down, then closes the toilet seat and invites the girl to do the same. "I won't look. I understand how uncomfortable you must be feeling."

The girl does as instructed, her son quiet in her arms. She pats his head the way a five-year-old pats her teddy bear in pretend consolation and presses her fingertips gently over his lips, which are bunched and ready to receive the nipple.

Even though Laird warned her not to get on a first-name basis with any of the children, Peggy wants to with this girl—just to diminish the horrible awkwardness of the situation. Laird claimed the community teaches its children to give false names, but as Peggy and the girl face each other with absolutely nothing in common, an exchange of false names would be something.

Peggy turns away to give the young mother some privacy. The waist of her slacks scoops below her tailbone, and she wonders if the girl notices her scorpion tattoo. Does she even know what a tattoo is? "Let me know when you're done, okay? If you have personal needs, I'll take your son and wait outside."

"I need help."

"Help?"

"With my son."

When Peggy turns back, the girl huffs and extends her arms until they lock at the elbows. The baby is balanced dangerously on the pads of her fingers. "I can't feed him." Her voice is pliant, like she's either about to wail or laugh hysterically. The baby gazes up at his mother through glassy eyes. She looks pointedly at her breasts. "I don't know how to make Bailyn take it. Bridger does that."

Peggy has an impulse to burst out of the bathroom and urge the children to retaliate, to run back to their mothers—to return to a world that wants them. Instead, she taps a finger three times below her right collarbone, on the small microphone Laird taped to her skin this morning.

"Bailyn and Bridger. Good work, Galvin." He sounds pleased. There's a crackle in the receiver in Peggy's right ear, and then silence and nausea.

The girl puts Bailyn on the floor between her white ballerina slippers and hugs her arms around her shins; she is vulnerable without her group. She is Project-F's best chance. Peggy's big chance. And while Laird and the other team members are doing the easy stuff, listening, taking notes, making plans, she has to engage with a teenager who doesn't know how to breastfeed her own baby. Bridger does that. Is Bridger the Father? The Prophet? Both?

The girl starts to weep. She squeezes her arms more tightly around her shins, fingers interlaced, hands bruised on the middle knuckles. Peggy lays a hand on the girl's shoulder and time both suspends and becomes elastic, the way it does when being held at gunpoint for the first time or walking in on your lover enjoying someone else's affections. Laird shouts into her ear. "Why so quiet, Galvin? What's happening? Keep her talking. Keep. Her. Talking!"

Bailyn squirms on the floor at his mother's feet, grabbing tiny fistfuls of his white blanket, opening and closing his mouth around them. As though being guided in a dream, Peggy reaches into her breast pocket for her kerchief. Before the girl can react, she touches the kerchief to her face and pats it dry. The girl smells of overripe bananas and rubbing alcohol. Her pulse labors through the vein across her forehead.

"There's a better way to give little Bailyn a bath, here," Peggy whispers. "You're goanna have to cry a lot more to get the job done right." It's the stupidest thing she could possibly say, but she has to connect with this girl, transform her from genetic horror show into human being.

"Bridger said you all were coming."

Peggy tucks the girl's hair behind her ears and examines the lobes, two hazelnut-sized knobs of loose, wrinkled flesh. She'll never be able to pierce her ears. Something so basic will never be an option for this girl. Blood tests aren't necessary to prove she's suffering from fumarase deficiency and carries the recessive gene; she has passed it onto her baby with the Dumbo ears. And what good is the proof? These two are as good as dead. CPS could prove all the children carry the gene, but it can't reroute their fate.

Laird rushes in once more. "Get her talking more about Bridger. Ask subtle questions to keep her on topic—*don't* bring up the Prophet."

"Is Bridger the Prophet?"

A series of curses in Peggy's ear.

The girl stands and smoothes the fabric of her starchy baptismal garment, peers down at her ankles to make sure they're covered, runs her hands over her face and re-braids her hair. Peggy feels hypnotized watching her preen in the mirror like a perfectly normal, well-adjusted teenager getting ready to meet friends at the mall.

The girl picks Bailyn up off the floor and kisses his forehead. "Bridger is my Prophet. We each have a Prophet."

The incongruity of her behavior from one moment to the next is so dramatic Peggy can't focus. It's Laird, buzzing madly in her ear, who enables her to respond. "You mean each person has a Prophet?"

"Only men are Prophets, and only mothers and daughters have Prophets. I would like to feed Bailyn now."

"Good, Galvin. Good! Keep her talking about Prophets. Keep that filthy vixen talking."

Laird boxes the air more vigorously than he does on Super Bowl weekend. After Galvin went into the bathroom, he stepped outside so he could speak to her without unsettling the children. No doubt their mutiny is as intolerable as their silence—worse than a B-rated horror movie. He has left the door ajar in case the situation in the basement becomes unmanageable, and when he peers in now he feels a desire to inflict pain on the children. The school-aged ones especially, who seem to be looking his way—all of them!—and daring him to hurt them. No punishment is too much for us, their collective eye proclaims. He turns away and kicks the desiccated rosebush around which he's been walking fast, tight circles; it explodes like bones from the impact of his Oxford shoe. He leans forward to thumb mud off his black trouser cuffs, pats the graying tufts at his temples, makes a mental note that it's time for a trim. To most women in their 20s, gray is sexy; a man who looks like a great-horned owl, however, is not.

He presses the headset microphone to his mouth. "What the fuck, Galvin? I don't hear anything."

In the same way he can't help hating the children for their ugliness, Laird can't help punishing Galvin for being who she is. The day he stopped by her office to invite her onto Project-F, he expected the woman to crawl out of her skin at the chance for an upstairs job. Everyone at CPS knows that basement jobs, like missing persons cases more than two years old, are terminal. And yet Galvin has been in that windowless office so long she commissioned her friend *Fréderique*, or something fruity like that, to paint an ocean scene mural facing her desk, an orange and pink sunset with a fleet of piping plovers skimming the saltwater surface. Better than seeing your boss's face every time you look up, or the clerks whom he's fucking, Laird supposes.

He presses the headset to his ears. "Galvin? Galvin, when you think you have something for me, sneeze twice, okay? Achoo-achoo. Tell me you hear me."

He waits for the blunt sound of finger-tapping, then steps back inside, staying by the exit door while he considers the scene before him: flies circling around the babies on the carousel, feasting on the opaque nasal discharge that volunteers have ignored all morning during diaper changes and feedings; CPS team members and volunteers shielding their noses with the backs of their hands, mouths dipping behind shirt collars. The breathing air has become toxic like in the basements of antique stores, old people's attics, and flophouses, but the children continue to hold their ground.

Laird recalls a cartoon that earned him a beating from the bullies in his second-grade class for closing his eyes during the scary parts. The villain stalked its prey (a rabbit, maybe?) disguised as a swirl of smoke. Whenever the rabbit stopped and sniffed around, the smoke thinned and disappeared, causing the rabbit's little pink nose to scrunch and twitch. Each time the rabbit went on its way, the smoke reappeared and took form more and more like whatever villain it actually was—wolf? hyena? panther? Until *POUF!* Bye-bye rabbit. The stench of these babies reminds Laird of the smoke villain. A mad, rotting animal creeping around the room.

The light bulb above the toilet is dark blue, the sort goth kids use to recreate the gloom of Nick Cave concerts. Its glow makes the young mother and her son look like Asiatic glassfish. Twenty minutes ago, Peggy could have left for lunch and returned unable to distinguish the pair from the group. Just another teenage girl and her infant. Noisier than the others, but otherwise as unique as two cans of Campbell soup. The shock of seeing children such as these for the first time wears off sooner than one expects; the psyche knows to accept certain horrors so the body can continue to operate.

"Get that baby fed, Galvin." Laird's voice sounds constricted.

Without thinking, Peggy asks, "Everything all right out there?"

Laird screams into her ear and she is volleyed between one disjointing reality and the other: the immediate of the bathroom, of Bailyn and his too-young mother, and that of what will become of her future with CPS after this day. She reaches for the wall and touches the girl by accident. The girl touches her back, her socketless eyes seeming to communicate that she understands, that she's sorry. Bailyn is back on the floor, his cries of hunger the only natural thing about this whole situation.

"Get me that baby, Galvin, and you'll never have a windowless office again," Laird croons.

If she succeeds in taking Bailyn from his mother and turns him over to the nurses and doctors waiting in the medi-van parked behind the church, the State will be in a position to begin making arrests, to rescue women and children from sexual slavery. If Project Fumarase succeeds, the State could become famous—nationwide, states have been plotting and planning and failing at capturing hosts of the recessive gene that first seized the public's attention in 2004 when a teenage mother snuck into a doctor's office with her newborn and begged someone to help the little girl breathe. The baby, just a few hours old, had been born with no nose, just two slits above her hare lip, and the slits had filled and clogged, causing her to suffocate. Over the next two weeks, a dozen more babies and children with varying degrees of bone-chilling physical and mental retardation were snuck to the office by trembling adolescent mothers, and the deficiency was named. Then, as suddenly as the young mother had appeared with her choking newborn, the entire community vanished. The only life that remained on the compound, once it was located, was a flourishing root vegetable garden. CPS has been tracking a group reported to be protecting the same gene discovered in the west of the country—the gene of "celestial will". Laird knows it, Peggy knows it, everybody on Project-F knows it, but without confessions and scientific evidence, they will have to release the children and Fathers, and then the group will vanish once more.

"Okay," Peggy says, rubbing her hands up and down the girl's arms in a vigorous, affectionate way. "Let's get this baby fed."

The girl smiles a broad, spontaneous smile, and just like that the trance is broken; she is missing gaps of teeth, and those she has are nubs the color of rubber bands, poking out of gums so tight with swelling they're almost white. Peggy's heart breaks, the girl reads it on Peggy's face, and intimacy evaporates faster than steam after an Arizona monsoon. The girl turns away, touching her hands to her arms where Peggy touched, mimicking the motion while considering the famished infant at her feet.

"I need to feed my son. Can you please undo my zipper?"

"Yes, of course."

So swiftly the girl has no time to change her mind, Peggy clasps her shoulders and turns her around. The girl allows herself to be manipulated without flinch or struggle, as though all vitality has left her and she is back on the compound, where women behave like robots. The zipper on the back of her dress is split open, but Peggy imitates the gesture of opening it properly nonetheless; maybe the girl will revive with some gentle physical contact. Peggy doesn't let her eyes train on the quarter-sized welts along the girl's spine. She has to tuck her thumb against her palm to keep from touching them; even though it doesn't matter whether they are hard of soft, she wants to know. She wants to touch them the way kids want to touch dead things. In all her imagined scenarios of how she would react to the horror of finally seeing the children, she imagined she would cry—the sadness of seeing them for real, these innocents sentenced to all varieties of awful existence because some madman believes keeping the blood "pure" will save *him* from eternal damnation. She's always imagined the sadness would consume her and she would fall to her knees. This is the most comforting thing about her windowless office job: no real horror to contend with. In the rare event a missing person is found, the body is barely bones; it's a blessing for everyone involved, as dust is so rarely the provenance of nightmares that keep people from sleeping soundly ever again.

Peggy shoves the girl aside and hurls into the toilet, deluging the cardboard tampon applicator in coffee and bile. As she heaves, the receiver dislodges from her ear and falls into the toilet. She lifts her hand, but her fingers won't open to trap the tiny black device; they defy her, coil into a fist, which punches her thigh over and over again, until she is crouched over, dry heaving, her tongue seizing from the strain, her eyes wide and wet.

Now she is alone with the girl.

A yellow school bus backs up behind the church. The driver honks and Laird comes running out, sweat pearled across his brow and upper lip. He directs the driver closer to the exit door and then waves his arms; the children will load more easily like this. They've grown belligerent in the last half-hour, since that girl and her baby left them. One of the pre-pubescent boys wet his pants on purpose, and a girl of about five picked her nose until it bled.

Laird walks up to the driver, a lissome brunette no older than 30 who should be playing volleyball on a beach or animating cruise ship activities instead. "Laird Fullerton, Assistant Director, Child Protective Services. Thank you for coming on such short notice." He makes sure to extend the hand showcasing his gold pinky ring with the black onyx monogram.

"Adina Michaels. If you wouldn't mind, I'd like to smoke a cigarette and then get back on the bus."

"Of course. We should be ready to leave soon." Laird extracts a gleaming, inscribed cigarette case from his pants pocket and flips open the lid. He smiles. "Please, try one. They leave a slightly sweet taste on the lips."

Adina chooses a cigarette from the center of the row, slides it neatly from the case and turns away to light it before Laird can offer his Zippo. "I'd really prefer not to see them, if you understand. I'm not involved, okay?" She exhales smoke as she talks, and then walks around to the other side of the bus.

Laird chooses a cigarette for himself, holds it up to appraise as though it's an expensive cigar, and then drops it unlit on the ground and destroys it with his Oxford. He hears the commotion in the basement, the sound of CPS and the church volunteers failing at getting the children to migrate to the bus. They're chanting again—"You're all going to Hell! You're all going to Hell!"— and they've formed a circle around CPS and the church volunteers. Laird watches from outside, pretending not to notice when one of his team members signals frantically above the chaos for backup. He can't bring himself to call for backup; his stomach is twisting all over again and he doesn't want to wretch in front of the bus driver. Not because she's hot, though. Because of principal. This is *his* project. Project Fumarase is his, and it will succeed.

He takes another cigarette from the case, lights it, holds his exhalation in his mouth and counts to ten before emitting a series of perfect blue smoke rings. He repeats this down to the filter and then flips open his cell phone. "Fullerton, here. I need some backup …yes, transport is here, but I need some squad—loaded."

Everything has been distilled to this moment for Peggy, whatever it is. That her future hinges heavily upon it bears no weight on the present.

The noise outside the bathroom is rocking the walls, quaking the foundation. She has no sense of how long it's taken her to steady herself, to stop the gagging and spinning and heart palpitations. The girl has been silent all this time, and Peggy expects she will turn to find mother and son gone. Instead, she finds the girl watching her levelly.

"I must go with them, but I would like you to help me feed Bailyn first."

Her edict makes Peggy shudder; how can so much composure exist in a person who has been denied the world? The girl's confidence wavers when she leans over to gather her son and the bodice of her dress falls to her waist. "I don't usually wear this. It fit me better before I was joined with Bridger." She balances her son precariously atop her palms once again. Bailyn senses the proximity of a food supply and his pouchy lips smack and suck at the air. The girl's eyes open in wonderment, then horror, and she thrusts her baby at Peggy.

Peggy draws Bailyn to her collarbone and pats his back. His mouth roots along the neckline of her blazer. "What have they done to you?"

The girl's front is a labyrinth of scar tissue. The tissue is so thick in places it looks like objects have been tunneled underneath. A scar that runs diagonally from her navel to under her left breast looks fresher than the others—a recently, hastily, sutured wound. The skin has barely fused together and appears crisp and faintly blue, though it's difficult to tell under the goth light. But the swelling is a definite sign of infection. On the girl's right side, in the spot where a nipple should be, is an older wound: a hole with an inch of tube sticking out of it. Yellowish fluid, Bailyn's overdue meal, oozes from the tube.

"You poor goddamn thing." Peggy lifts Bailyn higher on her shoulder and embraces the girl.

Outside the bathroom, Laird cracks his authority like a bullwhip, but the project will ultimately register as a failure. He knows it, in the way he's already begun to make everyone pay. Peggy hears it as the children are rounded up with police batons. The frenzy is reaching into the bathroom, and she knows time is up. They have run out of time, the girl, Bailyn, herself. She has accomplished nothing: The baby is unfed, the girl has made no confession, and she will be jobless at the start of next week. Perhaps CPS will order her to pay a contractor to paint over her sunset mural.

"I want to help you," she speaks into the top of the girl's head. "I wish I could help you." She teases a knot from the girl's long braid, tightens her arms around the bare torso and rocks back and forth, side to side; the girl hiccups, then begins to rock with her.

"Do you know what He told me, the day Bailyn was born?" she asks, lifting her head to press a cheek against Peggy's, mixing her tears with Peggy's the way some people mix blood.

Her scent, under that of unwash, is of limes. Bright green limes, full and healthy, and Peggy entertains a desperate fantasy. She imagines the girl standing beside her at the kitchen counter while she explains how limes can flavor almost any meal in the most delightful way. *You can marinate fish in lime juice, squeeze some on a bowl of white jasmine rice, or—now don't tell Him I said this!—drop a wedge into your vodka on a hot summer day.* "What, sweetheart? What did He tell you the day Bailyn was born?"

The girl reaches up with both hands to cradle Bailyn's head. "'Karaleen,' he said to me, 'as your Father, you both will always be protected as long as you lay with me and pray every night. They won't treat you nice out there because you are special. You are on this earth for bigger reasons.'"

Karaleen pulls away and takes her son; her movements are soft, swift, confident. Bailyn squawks loudly and gazes up at his mother with a tiny baby smile. Peggy nods, agrees to something she can no longer find a reason to contest, and gives Karaleen space—it's the only thing she can give.

"Maybe you are special," Karaleen says. "It was nice to know you."

She waits for Peggy to open the door, even though it was never locked, then breathes in the chaos before her and hugs Bailyn to her chest. Her group is loading the bus, and she will follow. Peggy stays behind and counts the number of scars on Karaleen's back, guesses how old they are, the reason for each one. Dazed-looking church volunteers cover their noses and unhook the babies from the carousel as Laird hollers and waves his baton over their heads.

ACKNOWLEDGEMENTS

Winter 2015: "Bleary" first appeared in *Gargoyle Magazine*, Issue 62.

Summer 2014: A slightly different version of "Bananas and Limes" first appeared as "Project Fumarase" in *New Madrid: Journal of Contemporary Literature*, Volume IX, Number 2.

October 2013: "A Marmalade Cat for Jenny" first appeared online with *Ampersand Review.*

October 2013: *The Poor Children* won grand prize for the Santa Fe Writers Project Awards Program for Fiction (judge David Morrell).

February 2013: *The Poor Children* was shortlisted for Salt Publishing's international Scott Prize (UK).

Autumn 2011: "Isabelle's Haunting" first appeared in *The Battered Suitcase: New Directions in Art & Literature*, Volume 4, Issue 2.

Spring 2010: "Layla" first appeared in *Short Story Journal* NS Volume 18, Number 1.

Thank you, mom and dad, for giving me the non-exchangeable gift of a writer's life. Thank you, Jonathan, for choosing to be my constant audience until death do us part. Thank you, Bianca Tredennick, for your enthusiasm and tireless eyes.

Thank you, SFWP team—Andrew Gifford, Karen Kovacs, and Shimrit Berman—for helping me establish my author-ness and for turning my manuscript into a book.

A book doesn't happen without dedicated readers—David Morrell, Sheila Lamb, Fred Leebron, Jonathan Dee, Naeem Murr, George Hovis, Pinckney Benedict, Elissa Schappell, Alice Lichtenstein, Michael Blaine, and Peter Such: Thank you.

And to Antonella Fratino, Rebeca Kuropatwa, Franco Zoccali, Matthew Eramian, Julia Campbell-Such, James Simon, Kynda Watt, and Michael Williams: You allowed me to thrust these stories upon you. You asked for more. You lured me out of my head with espresso and pastries. You are memorialized in the pages of this book and in my heart.

Bianca Tredennick

ABOUT THE AUTHOR

The Poor Children won grand prize for the 2013 Santa Fe Writers Project Literary Awards Program for Fiction (judge David Morrell). Earlier that year, the collection was shortlisted for SALT Publishing's international Scott Prize (UK). April's first novel, *Gentle*, was a finalist for the 2014 Molly Ivors Prize for Fiction, and a Semi-Finalist for the 2014 William Faulkner-William Wisdom Creative Writing Competition. April is Managing Editor of *Digital Americana Magazine*, and she teaches creative writing at State University of New York at Oneonta.

www.april-l-ford.com

A NOTE FROM THE PUBLISHER

Thank you for purchasing this title from the Santa Fe Writers Project (**www.sfwp.com**).

I started publishing because I love books. I publish titles that I would buy, and that I want to see on the shelves, regardless of genre. SFWP's mission is not about creating a catalog that the accountants can get behind. The mission is one of recognition and preservation of our literary culture.

I encourage you to visit us at www.sfwp.com and learn more about our books and our mission.

Happy reading!

Andrew Nash Gifford
Director
@sfwp

Santa Fe Writers Project